TRIUMPH

TRIUMPH

S. L. BENELLI

TRIUMPH

iUniverse books may be ordered through booksellers or by contacting:

iUniverse
1663 Liberty Drive
Bloomington, IN 47403
www.iuniverse.com
1-800-Authors (1-800-288-4677)

ISBN: 978-1-4917-8034-3 (sc)
ISBN: 978-1-4917-8035-0 (e)

Library of Congress Control Number: 2015917767

Print information available on the last page.

iUniverse rev. date: 11/04/2015

TABLE OF CONTENTS

CHAPTER 1

BEHIND BARS

Ray sat behind the table in the interrogation room. He had seen *Cops* on the television hundreds of times, and he knew what was coming next. He knew that his every move was being recorded and that everything he said would be used against him if the State had the chance. As he gathered his thoughts, the door opened and a detective walked in, followed by his partner.

"Mr. Jordan, I am Gustavo Real and this is my partner Francisco Ramos. Please call us Gus and Frank."

Ray nodded and extended his hand but the detectives chose to simply nod back and sit down across the table.

"Mr. Jordan, please tell us in your own words what happened out there today."

"I remember that we were walking to the movie house. We were crossing a street and then my wife was killed. I remember reaching for my pistol and then I was in a fire-fight. I don't remember much more until I kind of came to my senses in the back of the police car."

"Sure, you forgot everything. Is that right, Ray?"

Ray instantly recognized that Gustavo was playing the part of the bad cop and answered, "No, sir. I remember plenty, but I am not so sure that I should be talking about it right now."

"So what are you going to do, lawyer up? Innocent people don't do that."

Ray responded, "I think smart innocent people do and I consider myself both."

Gus gestured to Frank and said, "OK, Frankie, why don't you show Mr. Jordan to the tank. Maybe, he will want to talk to us later." On the way to the holding cell, Francisco looked at Ray with empathy and explained that he was there primarily to help Ray and to explain his situation to the state attorney. Francisco was filling his role as the good cop and was hard at work trying to gain Ray's confidence.

Ray was shown to the holding cell and left alone to wrestle with his thoughts for a short while. The cell was like a casino at six a.m., empty except for one or two patrons.

After some time passed, Ray heard the magnetic lock on the door just before it opened. Two uniformed officers escorted a good-natured drunk into the holding area. Ray listened as the drunk flip-flopped his way to the wall across the room. The drunk accompanied Ray and a sleeping vagrant who lay horizontal on the graffiti-laden steel bench that ringed the green concrete cell. Ray continued to stare at the floor between his feet. After a few minutes, he lifted his head and saw a cartoon of a man looking at him from across the room.

"Name's Doug," smiled the large, sunburned local. His clothes were shabby and faded from the sun, and his belly filled out the bottom of his shirt; small patches of hairy skin peeked out from the holes and under the bottom. "It's early, the place will start filling up after happy hour. What are you in for?" His manner and behavior indicated that he had been there before and was pretty comfortable with the routine. Ray didn't feel like having a friendly conversation and tried to ignore the man and returned to his study of the concrete between his shoes. "Time will pass a lot quicker if you talk to someone," Doug said persistently.

Knowing that Doug was right, Ray spoke, "Gunfight."

Doug recoiled and said, "Whoa, I didn't expect that! You look like a straight arrow, not a gunfighter. Me, I go to the bar to have a couple of drinks and there she is. My ex-wife sitting there, laughing it up with my drinkin' buddies. When I sit down she starts in, she doesn't say hi or nothing, she starts acting just like she did when we were married. I put up with her crap for an hour or so then she really got her ovaries in an uproar so I ordered a round and dumped my beer on her head to cool her off. It was all fun and laughs until some big dude that I didn't know started pushing me around. The next thing I know, he is getting a facial with my frosty mug and the cops are loading me into the car. Head cuts really bleed a lot, I think it scared him. I guess he didn't feel so big after saying hello to Mr. Stein."

Even though Ray felt terrible, he couldn't help but crack a smile at the tale that Doug had told. "The name is Ray, I am glad to meet you. I am afraid that I will be stuck here in Miami for a long time. I was told that two of the people I shot have died."

After noticing that Doug's jaw had dropped open, Ray continued, "They killed my wife. The bastards killed my wife. We lived together for 40 years and they took her away in a moment."

"Sounds like self-defense to me," followed Doug.

"That is the way I see it too, but there are a lot of conflicting opinions about my case. A lot of political correctness is in play. My chances of receiving a fair trial here seem pretty remote."

The magnetic lock buzzed again and the jailer asked Doug to follow him to another room. As he stood up, Doug looked at Ray and said, "Stay strong, brother. I wish my wife would have been good enough to fight over." The door closed with a kachunk and Ray was once again left by himself with his thoughts.

Ray was alone, a thousand miles from home and without a friend. He questioned his mind, wondering if scenes like these would be his future and what life would be like without Caroline. He reflected back to her youth and remembered just how beautiful she was and what great instincts she had when times were hard or when he was sad or despondent. She was the eternal optimist, the kind of mate who would nudge a man to greatness. She had always been there as a trusted friend and advisor. She was more than his wife; she had been his partner in life.

He closed his eyes and tried to block out the piercing glare from the fluorescent light fixtures that hung naked from the ceiling. He wondered what sickening event would come next and then after that, what would happen. He asked himself, *What would Caroline say now? What would she do?* It was all new to him. He, after all, was a law-abiding man. Surely the police and the State would understand that he was on their side.

He continued to lament the events of the day and his mind began to drift back in time to just two weeks before, a time when he was content, a time when he was happy, a time when he was free.

CHAPTER 2

GATHERING AT THE RANCH

As he cleared the rise in the road, Ray could see that one of the guests had arrived. His big Paint mare Lena let out a snort, as she could see the barn in the distance. He laid the horsehair rein against the left side of her neck and guided her to a better vantage point where he recognized a familiar red car parked in front of the big house. He watched as several people moved from the front door to the car and back. He smiled, thinking that they resembled ants hard at work as they shuttled themselves back and forth carrying luggage and brightly-colored packages. It would be good to see his son Danny and his family.

A drop of sweat rolled down his back, which reminded him that he still had a bit of work to finish up before he could welcome the early arrivals. The smell of damp leather and the sweat-soaked saddle blanket reminded him that his big black mare had put in a hard day as well and needed a bit of care before she could be turned loose with her friends in the near pasture. Ray had spent the last few hours checking the fence line on one of his far pastures. He had a pretty good idea that the wire was in good repair and he could have done the job far quicker and easier in his Ford pickup truck, but doing it on horseback gave him a chance to see his place through a much more natural eye. Riding his longtime

5

traveling companion, a uniquely marked Paint horse, added spice to the mundane chore and it gave Ray a chance to slow down and drink in the natural beauty that surrounded him. It was possible to ride up on a majestic elk or eagle without disturbing them as they went through their daily routine. It also gave him a chance to avoid the excitement and activity that surrounded the preparation of their fortieth wedding anniversary party that was scheduled for the following night.

Hector emerged from the barn with his hands held high to block the sun from his eyes. He motioned to Ray in a way that indicated that he had something to say.

As Ray rode closer, he looked down and Hector began to speak, "Nice ride, boss?"

"Yes sir it was, it never gets old. Next time why don't you saddle Prima or Deuce and we'll do it together."

Hector said, "I would like that too. We both are so busy with our own jobs these days that we don't get much of a chance to work together anymore, and I miss it."

"Me too, Hector, me too. We were a pretty good pair in our day, weren't we?"

Hector nodded as he pointed to the covered storage area and said, "Miss Carol wants all the sweaty tack put in the horse trailer."

"Thanks Hector, I'll meet you there," said Ray.

The barn hadn't been cleaner since its first day of operation. Hector had moved all the horses to a nearby pasture and pressure-washed the barn floor, relocated all of the bales of hay, and painted the place in anticipation of the barn dance that was taking place the next night. Ray looked at Hector as they neared the trailer and said, "I'll be glad when this deal is over."

As he swiveled to the ground, he unfastened his mecate and rolled a loop around a rail. He began to strip the cinch on his saddle when Hector offered to remove the remaining tack and brush down the horse so that Ray could greet his son and his son's family a little sooner. As Ray grabbed his saddle bags he said, "Thank you, Hector. I appreciate all the hard work you have put in."

Hector nodded as he held the big mare with a lead rope around her neck. After a quick brushing and cool down, he removed the vaquero bosal and led her to the near pasture to join her friends.

Ray knew Hector well, actually to the point of being able to read his mind; after all, they had worked together for more than 30 years, back to the early days of OSI in California.

CHAPTER 3

IN THE BEGINNING

Ray Jordan was a damn good welder. He had a head for building things out of steel, so when he found himself with a wife and a child on the way at twenty-two years of age, he started to make things. First, he worked as a subcontractor for a few of the fabrication shops and small manufacturing firms that dotted the San Fernando Valley, and then he moved on to small contracts for big companies like Disney, Paramount, and Atlantic Richfield. As time passed, Ray was able to buy five acres of dirt and later, a metal building. Eventually, he started Oilfield Services Incorporated, a small company that made custom and unique parts for Schlumberger and other big players in the oil business.

Hector showed up shortly after the first metal building was finished. He was a tall man, roughly six foot, and very slender, about 175 pounds. He was always on time and put in a hard day's work each and every day. Hector started as a field worker, helping with the installations and meeting with the customer representatives on the job site. As a first-generation American, he had studied diligently to master the English language. This proved to be valuable to the company because OSI hired many minorities and Hector was able to motivate and instruct them well. He was quick-witted and likable. He also had the ability to solve problems without supervision.

Hector became the field boss as the company grew, as he could communicate with the crew in both English and Spanish. Ray had always considered Hector to be a trusted partner in the company and had increased his salary every year until he was solidly into the six figures. Ray liked the fact that Hector was decisive and took a good deal of the responsibility off of his shoulders. Hector had provided his two children with good college educations and purchased a nice ranch-style home in an upscale Burbank neighborhood for himself and his wife, Lupe.

As the years turned into decades, Hector remained a constant at OSI until one day in June of 1997.

Hectors cell phone vibrated and brayed like a donkey.

"Hello, Hector, this is Ray. I need to have a word with you back here in my office."

"Is everything OK?" Hector asked.

"Yeah, there is nothing wrong, but we are having a meeting of the group leaders and I want you to be here. Let Johnny run the crew until you come back tomorrow," Ray said.

"OK, I'll head right in. I should be there in about an hour. Is there anything you need for me to pick up on my way back to the shop?"

"No thanks, we are good here. Just drive safe, OK?"

Hector acknowledged Ray's warning by saying, "Sure thing, I will leave right away."

After Hector arrived, the intercom barked out the names of the shop manager, the assistant office manager, the sales manager, the production manager, and the personnel director. They were instructed to come to the anteroom next to Ray's office for a meeting.

The anteroom was a silent oasis inside the busy and noisy fabrication plant. Its green walls were double sound insulated to block out the din from the production area, and the hefty solid core doors closed tightly.

Caroline sat in a chair located to the right side of Ray and greeted each person with a smile and a nice compliment as they entered the room. It was just her way. She always tried to keep a friendly and optimistic tone in the entire office. After everyone found a seat around the polished mahogany table, Ray began to explain why he had called this unexpected meeting.

"Last night, Caroline and I made an agreement in principal with Mason Petroleum Services to sell our share of the company to them. We were prohibited from discussing this sale with anyone outside of our lawyer and a few others in the Mason organization because they wanted all of my personnel to be in place when they took over the operation of the company."

A quiet buzz erupted in the meeting room as the employees shifted, sighed, and reacted to the news.

"I want you all to know a few things," Ray continued, in an effort to reassure his staff. "First, I am telling you at my earliest possible opportunity, and secondly, I have highly recommended to them that everyone who works here should remain at the jobs that they are filling right now. I know that you must have some more questions, so please fire away."

"What about our jobs, Ray? What do you expect to happen?" asked Linda, the personnel director. Her expression was unusually serious and the furrows in her brow expressed a mind that was insecure and troubled.

Ray paused and rubbed the stubble on his chin.

"Well, my friends, I expect that they will keep all of the production workers in place. I think the only jobs that may be in jeopardy will be the ones you folks occupy. Like I said, I have given glowing reports on every one of you, but I also know that they have usually placed family members into many of the key positions at their other plants. I have made sure that your possible departure was written into the contract."

When Ray ended, Caroline, sensing panic and despair, looked at Linda and continued, "Ray has stipulated that Mason must keep all of you on the payroll for at least 180 days at your current wage or they must compensate you two weeks' pay for every year that you have worked here as a minimum severance package. Since all of you have worked here at least ten years, the cash buyout should give you a pretty nice cushion if you do have to find employment somewhere else. We promise to do what we can for each and every one of you."

Linda did a mental calculation, and then she seemed somewhat relieved. She smiled at Caroline and said, "Thanks boss, I knew that you would."

"What are you planning on doing after you retire?" asked the sales manager.

"Caroline and I have purchased a fair sized piece of land near Daniel, Wyoming, and we plan on moving there and raising a few head of cattle and maybe a few horses."

"That sounds nice. Can I come up and visit?" the sales manager asked.

"Any time, all of you, any time," Ray said. He smiled and gestured with a sweeping motion of his hand while Caroline smiled and nodded in agreement.

The shop manager followed by asking, "When will you be leaving?"

Ray looked at his notes and responded, "The target date for the transition is mid-August and we are obligated to be here until then." Ray looked around the room and asked, "Any more questions? That is about it, a short meeting with a lot of important things being said. Keep in mind that my office is always open to any of you if you think of anything later on. Hector, I would like you to stay behind for a few minutes if you don't mind."

Hector nodded and waited as the rest of the people left the room behind Caroline. Some of the people already had their cell phones out and were calling their spouses or figuring their potential severance bonus on the calculator.

Ray sat down next to Hector and looked into his puzzled looking face and said, "Hector, my friend, I wanted to tell you this man to man. I know for a fact that your position is going to be given to Mr. Mason's nephew. The kid just got out of college with a degree in engineering and the old man wants him to learn the operation from the ground up. The old man told me that he felt that the field supervisor would be the best place for his nephew to learn the business. He also made a few comments about your salary that made me think that he didn't want to keep you on, at least at that rate."

Hector was silent throughout the meeting. He looked up with sad eyes and told Ray, "This is really a surprise, Ray. Man, I had no idea that this was coming."

Ray asked, "Are you OK financially?"

"Oh yeah, no problem. I just don't know what I am going to do when I don't have a job to go to in the morning."

Ray paused and posed the question, "What do you think about moving to Wyoming to work with me on the ranch?"

Hectors eyes grew wide as he said, "Are you serious? Move to Wyoming and chase cows?"

"Dead serious. I have already spoken with Caroline about it," Ray said.

"Wow, that would be a big step, but, by God, I'll consider it. I will talk to Lupe and get back with you."

"Listen, Hector, here are a few things for you to consider. If you go with me, you will live in the foreman's house rent free, and I will pay you a fair wage to boot. Not to mention the severance package that Mason gives you, the equity in your house, and any savings that you have. With your seniority and the increased value of your house, you will leave here a rich man. The place is peaceful and the work will be a lot less stressful than living and working here. Beside that, Hector, I trust you and I personally would like to continue working with you."

"Thank you, boss, I appreciate what you are saying. I just need a little time to consult with my bride and the boys."

Ray smiled and said, "Sure, take the rest of the week off and head home. I'll see you on Monday, amigo."

Four days later, Hector pushed his way through a group of corporate executives that crowded into Ray's office. He staked out a place in an obscure corner of the office and tried to catch Ray's eye as he detailed a few of the contracts that were in the pipeline. The execs listened as Ray talked of price and quantity, hours needed for the production of each item, the final product inspection process, and the transportation, installation and maintenance after the sale. They asked his opinion of changes that they had in mind that were in use in some of their other facilities. Ray listened to their ideas and gave them his best advice even though it didn't always agree with the consensus in the room. When Ray caught sight of Hector, Hector said, "When you get a few minutes, I would like to talk." Ray nodded and returned his attention to the other men in the office.

At about eleven forty five, the group of executives began to change the conversation from the details of the business to where can a fellow get a good meal around here? Ray directed them to a local home-style restaurant and a couple of chain outlets that were not far away.

"Are you coming, Ray?" one asked.

"No thanks, I have some private business to attend to so I'll just grab a bite in the break room or inside my office," Ray answered. "That will also give you fellows a chance to talk freely over lunch."

After the men had piled into their rented Lincoln and headed out the driveway, Hector walked into Ray's office. He held two steaming-hot homemade burritos wrapped in aluminum foil. With a calloused hand, he handed one to Ray and sat down. As they made small talk and prepared to eat, Caroline walked in with a couple of bottled waters and said, "I have eaten Lupe's burritos, so I think you will need a couple of these to put out the fire," and as quickly walked out, closing the door.

Between bites, Ray looked at Hector and said, "So what is the decision?"

Hector smiled and said, "We have decided to go." Then he added, "This place just chokes you. There are too many rules and too many people who don't respect your things and your being."

"I have to confess, Hector, we started construction on the ranch foreman's house after our conversation last week. I hope twenty-four hundred square feet of log cabin will suit you and the missus."

"That will do fine. That's the same size as the house we have now and since the children have moved away, we have a ton of room," Hector said.

"Your home is located about five hundred feet away from my place and we have a sixteen-stall barn in between. I think that it is close enough to be convenient and far enough away to still give each of us some privacy and some space. Construction will be finished in about five months, so I think you better get busy and get your place sold. We are scheduled to turn over the keys to the company on August the tenth, so I'll be heading north shortly thereafter. I have a pending contract on my house, and my house up there is almost finished, so I won't be staying here any longer than necessary."

Looking at Hector, Ray continued, "I have an idea. Your place won't be ready until early February and it should be pretty damn cold by then. Why don't we do this? Why don't you figure on leaving California the same time as we do? You can stay with us in the big cabin and help direct the finishing touches on your place. You can put your household goods in storage and have them shipped out after the house is finished. It will give us a chance to start setting up the ranch and buying some stock."

Hector nodded and got a distant look in his eye.

"I like the idea. When I was a kid back in Mexico, my parents had a mule that my brothers and I used to ride. It will be good to get back to the smells and sounds of nature after living here for so many years. It is easy to forget the past when you get wrapped up in making the almighty dollar. All we see are people, people, people, and maybe a domestic dog or cat once in a while. I think a big animal like a horse or a cow is good for your soul. Working with them gives you a kind of peace and trust that you rarely get from other people. You know there aren't even any empty lots left for the kids to play in. They have to go to the city parks and you know who hangs out there. Too many two-legged mules, eh boss?"

There was a pause while the men ate their foil-wrapped burritos.

As they neared the end of the meal, Hector continued, "I'll let you know for sure tomorrow, but it sounds real good to me right now. I know Lupe will want to break the news to her sister, now that we have a date."

"Sure thing," Ray answered. "Hey, tell your in-laws that you will have four bedrooms in your place, so if you want them to visit, there will be enough room."

"I'll have to think on that one for a while," Hector said as he smiled.

Later, Ray met with the new plant manager and a couple of suits from Mason Petroleum's main office. He gave them some recommendations and advice regarding Hector's replacement. He once again detailed the standard operating procedures that he had used so successfully for more than 30 years, but down deep he knew they would make some changes that would turn his shop that was run like a family into just another place to work.

Ray was good at taking an interest in his people and their families. Each year at Christmastime, Ray would buy all of his employees a large turkey, and in the spring they would have a company picnic just to let the employees get to know each other outside the shop floor. He technically had one more week remaining on his contract to stay on, but he suggested to all of the new management team that they try to run things without Hector, Caroline, and himself, just to make sure that they would have a smooth transition. It also meant that they could prepare for their move to Wyoming.

CHAPTER 4

LEAVING CALIFORNIA

The plane tickets had been purchased, a Wyoming bank account was established, and a new Ford diesel pickup was to meet them at the airport. Ray had visited the site in Wyoming on a couple of occasions and used a rental car for transportation, but he knew that a big truck would be needed to see the corners of his land. He called his local Ford dealer in California, a guy who had sold Ray dozens of trucks over the past 30 years. He arranged a split sale with a dealer near Jackson for a King Ranch Special.

The alarm on the intercom shouted the local news to Ray and Caroline at five a.m. They had awakened some time earlier and had been pillow talking about the big day that lay ahead. With hearts beating like thunder, they made morning coffee and settled down to some bacon and eggs in their almost-empty home.

Caroline looked across the kitchen counter and said, "You know, we have been at this thing for a long, long time and in just about four hours, we are going to close on a twenty-eight million dollar deal. I know we have to give the governor and the president their ransom, but we are still going to walk away a lot better off than what we had when we got started.

"We meet with the attorney at eight," she continued, "and then we go to the title company for the closing. Man, life is really going to change!" They tidied up the house for the new owners and locked the front door for the last time as they headed down the driveway towards their new life in Wyoming.

They sat across the table from the executives from Mason Petroleum Services and exchanged pleasantries. The clerk walked in and began passing papers from side to side and indicating signatures here, here, and there until the stack of papers had been completely shuffled and then returned to its regular order. The entire transaction was quite easily done and seemed painless for everyone who surrounded the table.

Soon the clerk returned into the room and handed Ray a cashier's check for $17,327,480.86. Estimated taxes had been paid to the state and federal government.

"We don't usually close on deals this big," the clerk said. "I want to thank you both for being so cooperative. It has been our pleasure to serve you."

Ray noticed that their cost had been over ten grand for that half-hour's work, but he kept quiet and figured that the cold bottle of water and the new ballpoint pen that bore the name of the title company was somehow worth the money.

He handed the check to Caroline and said, "If it's OK with the boss, well then it's OK with me." Everyone laughed to release the tension and then began to file out of the room.

After taking Caroline home, Ray returned one last time to the shop to deliver his company car. He hitched a ride home with one of the longtime employees who happened to be the pickup and delivery driver.

The driver looked at Ray and said, "I hate to see you go. I think things will be changing. There is talk about these new guys freezing our wages for a couple of years."

Ray shook his head and said, "Give them a chance. You know they probably won't do things as I did, but they also have the resources to give you a lot more in fringe benefits. Who knows what they might do. Just give them a chance."

"Well, good luck to you, boss."

"You too, Al, God bless you," Ray said as he stepped from the truck and waved an exaggerated goodbye.

A few hours later, the yellow cab pulled to the curb at the passenger drop-off location at Los Angeles International Airport, and then Ray and Caroline stepped onto the busy walkway and headed into the terminal building. Ray heard some profanity being bantered between three teenage boys as they jostled and shoved each other down the concourse. Ray looked up as one of the boys who had been pushed bumped into an elderly woman and knocked her to the tile floor. They chided each other with more profanity as they each blamed the other for the incident, but none of them stopped to help the lady in need. Several travelers passed right by the floundering woman in their myopic rush to or from their planes.

As they neared the scene, Ray put down his suitcase to kneel down and ask the woman if she was all right. She said that she was not injured seriously, but she was having a hard time getting back on to her feet. Ray offered to help her up and she accepted by extending her frail arms to him. As Ray began to help the lady right herself, a traveler rushing to his gate muttered at them for blocking the walkway. After righting the elderly lady and escorting her to a safe place, Ray looked at Caroline and said, "Hector was right. I think it's time we leave this place. There is too much disrespect around here for a decent man to tolerate anymore."

Ray picked up his lonesome suitcase with a few clothes and toiletries and continued to the gate. Everything else had been shipped to their new log house and a crew was set to meet them first thing in the morning to arrange the furniture and set up the house. The contractor had received a Certificate of Occupancy a week before and had stocked the kitchen with some basic food items and disposable dinnerware. He also had beds and linen set up in the master and guest bedrooms, and the adjacent baths were already supplied with toiletries, fresh towels and mats.

Hector paced back and forth in front of the windows overlooking the tarmac, while Lupe smiled in excitement.

She greeted them with a hug and said, "What a fantastic adventure!"

Caroline grabbed her hand and spoke, "Yes, indeed it is!"

Hector noticed Ray's arrival and walked forward to meet him. He said, "I was worried. I thought you would never get here. We're supposed to check in real soon."

"Thanks Hector, I'm glad you care."

"Yeah I care, mainly because you have the keys to the house," Hector joked.

"What is that supposed to mean?" Ray bantered back.

"It means if you miss the plane, Lupe and I will have to sleep outside with the coyotes when we get there."

"Oh, that," said Ray, and then the two men laughed.

After checking their bags, they stood in line for the TSA routine. The inquisitor asked Hector a few personal questions and Ray fought off the temptation to speak out. He let Hector handle the overweight government employee with some wit and intelligent answers. Soon, they entered the first-class section and sat down in row six for a flight to Denver and a hop to a grass field near Jackson. The estimated time of arrival was four in the afternoon.

Chapter 5

Early Days at the Ranch

Charlie Willett, the contractor, waited at the side of the grass landing strip at the local airport. The pilot spotted the new pickup and taxied the craft to a location adjacent to the truck's rear door. After the motor was shut down, Charlie greeted them as they stepped down from the aircraft with a heavy handshake and a big smile.

"I took the liberty to drive your new truck out here to pick you up because mine was full of tools and sawdust," Charlie said.

Ray threw the bags into the back of the truck and they all got in for a ride to the homestead. Lupe remarked about the desolation and the quietness of the place and noted that it was in stark contrast to the din and congestion of Los Angeles.

Charlie laughed to himself and replied, "If you think this place is lonesome, then you haven't seen anything yet!"

They soon drove out of Jackson, then south towards the little town of Daniel, and after about thirty minutes, Charlie pulled to the side of the road and pointed into the distance.

"Can you see that pile of rocks over there? That is where your land starts."

He drove about one quarter mile up the road and cleared a hill. Down below was a pair of beautiful log homes situated on a stunning rise with a fabulous barn in between. The barn was finished and it was easy to see the detail that Charlie had perfected. A weather vane that was made into a big brass horse topped the steeple. The hitching posts and signage that identified the barn as the Rockin' Lazy J were top notch.

"Well, Charlie, the photos you sent me did not do justice to your work. If the house looks as good as the barn," Ray said.

Lupe gasped at the sheer beauty of the scene. They saw two beautiful log homes, a river in the distance, and a creek nearby.

Hector quietly said to himself, "Man, what a place."

Ray replied, "Yes, it's quite a place, and starting tomorrow, we have to fence it."

They pulled up to the paved entry, exited the truck and walked up the steps that were constructed from logs sectioned in half to a broad front porch that surrounded the entire house. The arched entry door was nearly eight feet high and almost four feet wide, with structural black iron supports that resembled half of a wagon wheel at the top. It was made from nearly three-inch thick cedar planks and closed like a bank vault.

Once they entered the home, the ceiling was open to about twenty feet and had the equivalent of a second home upstairs. It was awe-inspiring. The logs glistened in satin finish and the triple-pane glass windows were massive. The view was nothing less than spectacular.

Charlie had done it right and cut no corners. He had even taken the time to have some dry firewood, a book of matches, and a few folding chairs available for the evening. The house had a massive stone fireplace made from rocks found in the nearby creek that had been smoothed by millions of gallons of water over many years. The firebox was almost six feet across and the fire brick were laid in a herringbone pattern with no shiners. There was also a soapstone-lined wood burning stove located near the kitchen. Charlie explained that in all of the homes this remote, a good wood burning stove was considered an essential for winter safety.

They moved from room to room and the remarks were increasingly complimentary. Charlie showed the ladies the pantry, which looked almost empty except for a few cans of food and the paper plates and plastic utensils that had been pressed into service for that night. He also mentioned that he had stocked the bathrooms with a few other important items and had even set out two new pairs of bath towels in case they wanted to wash off the smog from California.

After going over a few technical details, Charlie said that he wanted to get home before dark so he was hitting the road. He checked to see if Ray's cell phone had a signal and said, "Call me if you have any problems. I'll be back in the morning."

As he fired up his dusty Dodge diesel, he leaned out the window and said, "I left you a gift in the fridge." Charlie then clattered away down the road. As the sound disappeared, they began to realize just how remote they were. The silence was broken when Hector quipped, "Do you think we need to lock up the truck?"

They all laughed, but the noise from the laughter was swallowed up by the vast stillness of the evening. They heard the sound of a dove, then a few crickets and a distant lonesome wolf. When they walked inside, they were home.

As the sun hit the horizon, the night got cool and dark quickly. The living room fire looked small in the huge firebox, but it took the chill from the air. The bottle of pinot noir that Charlie had left in the refrigerator helped everyone stay warm on the inside. They opened and warmed up a big can of Dinty Moore beef stew and, after it was divided into quarters, covered it in Saltine crackers. As they sat in the glow of the fireplace drinking French wine from plastic cups, they all agreed that this meal was better than any they had eaten in any Los Angeles five-star restaurant. After some quiet reflection, they went to their rooms for the night.

Chapter 6

Nearly Ten Years Later

Ray walked into the mudroom and could see his son Danny and his wife Jan had arrived. They were in the living room talking to Caroline about the party. He stripped off his gun leather and chaps. He placed his Colt .38 Super out of sight on a high shelf just inside the living room door.

"Have you guys settled in yet?" he asked.

"Yeah, we are unpacked and ready to have a good time," Jan said.

"Well, I expect that to happen. We have a side of beef ready for the pit, and Hector has the barn all lit up and ready. We stocked the bar with a case of hard liquors and a keg of beer on ice."

There were some hugs all around, and then Ray sat down to join the conversation. "We have a catering service coming in to man the bar and take care of the cooked food. We said we would provide the beef and drinks and they are doing all the rest," Ray said.

"How big is this thing going to be?" Danny asked.

"We expect about 75 people, which is pretty much everyone around here. The sheriff is expected to drop by for a social call and we have invited a couple of political heavyweights as well. It is really good to see you all. Where are the kids?"

"Upstairs. They should be down pretty soon."

Just then Ray heard his granddaughter ask, "Hey Grandpa, are you having a band at this thing or just playing music from a CD?"

Ray answered, "We got these guys out of Jackson that are really good. They are called flatbed musicians. They have a rigged-up old flatbed truck that is all set up. They drive in, plug it in and start playing. It's a great deal, no setting up and no packin' up. Works really well if it doesn't rain."

Danny and Jan both worked as professors at the state college in Chadron, Nebraska. They met as students and had been married for more than ten years. Danny studied chemistry, while Jan had acquired a Juris Doctor degree; she worked at a couple of local law firms and then chose to join Danny at the college as a law professor. Despite the fact that Jan was from the northeast, Ray always liked her. She was spunky and not afraid to get her hands dirty. She also took damn good care of her family.

After Ray had showered off the sweat and dust, he went for a walk with his son Danny and his grandson Julian. They walked to the near pasture where Ray had moved his seasoned ranch workhorses. With a wistful look, Ray said, "I sure missed my calling."

"What do you mean, Grandpa?" Julian asked.

"If I would have known how much I enjoy working with these horses when I was a young man of twenty-two, I probably would have been a cowboy instead of a welder."

Ray put his arm around his grandson Julian and said, "Remember that, son, learn a lot about a lot of things then make your choice carefully, because these middle age years, the ones where you have all the responsibility and all the pressure, well, they go by really fast. Who knows? If I hadn't been a good welder, I probably wouldn't have got rich, and if I hadn't got rich, I probably would have gone to my grave not even knowing about these beautiful beasts. Life's funny, so get on the right path early and you won't have to waste a lot of time catching up. Also remember, they can't pay you enough money to work at a job that you hate. I always liked my work at the shop, but I love it here. I guess it is right for me at this time in my life. Danny, I hope you guys like it here and would someday like to live here."

"Well you know dad, it's a long way from anywhere and ..." Danny began.

"Don't say any more, just know that you always have a place here if you want it," Ray said. Shaking Julian's shoulder, Ray said, "You too, young man, this can be your place as well. This isn't a real big operation, and there really isn't enough room to get really big, but a section of land can be decently profitable for a family business. We have a fairly productive cow-calf operation with this good line of Aberdeen Angus. Our horse breeding business is really good. We have acquired a double homozygous Paint stallion with heavy foundation bloodlines and we are producing the nicest line of American Paint horses in this part of the country. We set off nearly three hundred acres of alfalfa hay and we have worked a deal with one of the local farmers to split the yield fifty – fifty ... Ah, damn it! You don't want to hear about business! It's just me; I always look at things like a business. It's just in the blood. You know boys, doing this makes you rich in a way you can't measure with money. It's simply good for your mental health."

Hector beckoned to the trio and they began to walk toward the barn. "Hector, as usual, you have made this place shine like a diamond," Ray said. Reaching into a small refrigerator in the tack room, the men opened three cervezas and one A&W root beer for Julian. They sat in a circle in some folding chairs enjoying the breeze through the center aisle of the barn. As the men began to laugh at each other with the kind of good-natured ridicule that is reserved only for the best of friends, Hector asked with seriousness, "Is there anything else you can see to do, boss?"

"No, Hector, I think you have it all covered. Everything looks great. Why don't you kick back until you can enjoy the party?" Hector then nodded, stood up, and took the last pull out of his bottle. With his bowed legs and walked over boots, Hector ambled to the edge of the barn, dropped his bottle into the empty trash can, and disappeared around the corner. The trio continued to catch up on the family gossip and news until they had finished their drinks, and then they walked to the house.

CHAPTER 7

THE ANNIVERSARY PARTY

The sun was still high when friends and neighbors started down the dirt road toward the barn. First there was a GMC one-ton, then a freightliner bobtail and several Fords. The clatter and smell of the diesels filled the air as the guests arrived. The barn filled with neighbors making small talk, mostly about what they were doing at each of their spreads, and the keg beer and liquor lubricated the conversation. A Pancho and Lefty CD played in the background. Caroline and Ray were busy shaking hands and greeting the arrivals as Danny and Hector exhumed the beef from the pit. One of the neighbors showed up with several pounds of cooked venison and smoked salmon for hors d'oeuvres and passed several plates to the early arrivals.

As sundown grew closer, a black Cadillac rolled up the dusty road. The car looked peculiar in the sea of heavy rigs that surrounded the barn. Senator Thorne emerged from the back seat with his young attractive trophy wife. They wore western shirts, jeans, and boots. Senator Thorne was a solid conservative voice in Washington. Ray and most of his neighbors had contributed heavily to his election. The liberals liked to say that he was named right because he was always a pain in the ass to them.

Ray and Caroline greeted the couple and introduced them to some others in the crowd while a horn honked and the flatbed musicians backed their custom 1938 Chevy flatbed into the barn.

Dinner was set up as the band started to play. The first few tunes were classic country. They were excellent musicians and covered Merle Haggard and Hank Jr. very well. After the guests were served dinner, the band took a break to give everyone a chance to talk. This also gave the musicians a chance to enjoy a bit of pit-cooked beef and beer. As dinner wound down, the slim bandleader went to the microphone and said, "We have had a request for some classic rock music." The announcement was greeted with mixed boos and yeas, but the band ignored the din and kicked off "I Know a Little" note for note of the Lynrd Skynrd classic. By the time they finished, the place was rockin'. Songs that followed were the best of Deep Purple, Marshall Tucker, Charlie Daniels, and the Allman Brothers. The band was superb and their music filled the night with vitality and humor.

Towards the end of the evening, Danny came to the microphone. He tapped a half-filled glass with a fork to get everyone's attention. He said that he had a gift for his folks. Danny explained that he and his absent brother had put together a gift for their parents.

Jan presented Caroline with a small box. As everyone watched, Caroline opened the box to reveal a Hawaiian shirt for Ray and some pink sandals for her. Along with the gifts was an all-expense-paid cruise to the Caribbean from Miami, Florida. Caroline smiled and looked surprised and said thank you and showed the gifts to the guests, while Ray stood there with an unhappy look on his face.

Ray found a chair at one of the empty tables and looked as though he was three thousand miles away. From time to time, he could be seen covering his eyes with his right hand like he had a headache. After a few minutes, he also made his way to the microphone and said, "It's late, we only have the band until eleven, and I don't have to tell any of you that tomorrow is a work day. Thanks to you all for coming, I hope you had a real good time."

As the band played "Sweet Melissa," the smell of diesel smoke filled the night air as one by one the neighbors headed home. Soon the band had unplugged, and the flatbed musicians were the last set of taillights going down the road.

Ray had trouble keeping his feelings from bubbling to the top. He had made plans to work on a big deal with one of his neighbors, plus it was time to auction off all of the calves and young horses. They had a roundup set for next week where the bull calves would be 'steered' and given their shots. It was a couple of hard days of work but it was, at the same time, a lot of fun and Ray was looking forward to it. Hector sensed that something was wrong and kept to himself.

As they cleaned up the tabletops and put the tables and chairs away, Ray grabbed a half-empty beer bottle and flung it in the trash, breaking several of the dead soldiers inside the barrel.

Caroline looked up and said, "All right, Ray, we know you are pissed. Don't make a fool of yourself."

Ray had drunk a little bit too much to be inhibited, so his words flowed without restraint. "What the hell were you thinking?" he said to Danny. "You know we live here on the edge of the wilderness because we like it here. What makes you think I want to go on some damn cruise?"

Caroline stepped between them and said to Danny, "We love the gift and we will go on the cruise."

Ray kicked at the ground and said, "Well it looks like you all have a pretty good handle on what we need to do around here so I think I'll just leave it with ya'. I'm done!" He turned from the group and stormed into the darkness towards the house.

The bedroom was dark as Caroline dressed for bed. She slipped under the covers and when she touched Ray, he acted as though she were a leper. He moved away and faced the wall with every muscle on edge.

Caroline sighed and said, "Things will look better in the morning."

It was quiet for a minute or two. Then from out of the silence, "Bull shit," punctured the inky air.

Chapter 8

The Morning After

As the bacon sizzled, Ray entered the kitchen to pour a cup of coffee and start his day. Danny and his family were still in bed.

Caroline asked, "Sleep well?" with a smile.

"Not worth a crap," Ray replied.

"You always tell me that you can't lose your head when working with big animals or you will get hurt, right?" she asked.

"Well yes."

"I think the same goes with people, Ray."

"Yeah, probably so. So?"

She laid a plate in front of Ray with two eggs cooked over medium and fried in bacon fat on top of a heaping pile of grits, with bacon and jellied toast on the side. Ray immediately began to feel better.

Between bites, Ray asked, "So when do we leave on this cruise deal?"

"It's supposed to be wheels up in three days from Denver, and we will be gone nine days. You will still have plenty of time to do the roundup. Danny and his family will stay here and help Hector until we return."

"You know Caroline, I would like it a whole lot better if I could be with the kids for nine days and let them help out with the branding and the roundup."

"I know, and maybe next year we can work on that, but this thing means a lot to the boys, so I want to do it."

"OK, I'll play along and I promise to make the best of it."

Danny entered the kitchen and said, "Well at least you're talking."

"Your mother's cooking will always tame the wild beast within. Sorry I snapped at you last night, son."

"No harm done. I should have considered your point of view when Rodney suggested it, so I'm partly at fault as well."

"I know your heart is in the right place and your mother tells me that we are going to have a good time whether I like it or not. You know, I haven't been to sea in a long time. Who knows? I might really enjoy it. Remember those all-day charters out of San Pedro? Or that time we went down to Mexico when you were twenty-one?"

"Yeah, that was a good time. We caught those big Bonita and you won the jackpot," Danny said. "We looked so grubby on the way back into the U.S. that they tossed the car at the border before letting us pass."

Ray smiled and responded, "Yes, I remember it well. I sure hope this cruise deal doesn't turn out to be a jackpot of a not-so-great kind."

Jan entered the kitchen and kissed Danny on the top of his head.

"That coffee sure smells good!" she said.

Ray looked up and said, "Good morning."

Jan smiled and asked, "Are you feeling better?"

Ray nodded, smiled and said, "Professor, I plead nolo contendere."

"Well all right then, you should be hitting the high seas real soon," she said.

"Hey Jan, can I carry a gun on this trip?" Ray asked.

"I think you can. Florida has a reciprocity agreement and the airlines transport them every day, but I don't think that you can bring one aboard ship. If you feel strongly about having a gun on the trip, you will have to check it in at the bus station, the hotel safe, or some other secure location while you are out to sea."

"You know I feel kind of naked without a piece nearby," Ray said.

Joking, Danny said, "It isn't that kind of cruise, Dad!"

Ignoring his son, Ray replied, "I think I will call the hotel and see if they will stow it for me while we are gone."

"Good thinking," said Jan. "They know that you will be coming back due to the reserve dates on your reservations. There shouldn't be a problem."

"The smallest thing I have is that old Colt 1903 that dad sent me when I was in Viet Nam. I think I may oil her up later today."

As Caroline kept the food and coffee cooking, Ray and Danny talked about what chores had to be done while he and Caroline were away.

"Be sure to check the water in the landlocked pastures every day," Ray said. "Hector knows the feeding schedules, so just do whatever he asks you to do. Do you know that you will have to get up a little earlier than you are used to?"

"I know, I'll make that sacrifice for you old folks."

"Keep it up, son. When those stalls fill with horse shit and Hector tells you to start raking, think of me sitting in a deck chair getting a tan and hoisting a cold beer. Old folks my ass."

Chapter 9

The Cruise

The Cessna 180 landed on the auxiliary runway adjacent to the Denver International Airport. An air caddy met them on the tarmac and hustled them and their baggage to the main terminal where Ray handed the agent an official form declaring a gun in the locked container. She read the paper and snapped another tag on that bag and sent it through to be loaded onto the aircraft.

They walked to the American Air Lines gate 38 and stood in line to be inspected by the TSA personnel. After waiting in line for thirty minutes, they finally got their turn to talk to the obese man in the white and blue uniform.

"Shoes?" he asked.

"Yes, I have some," Ray answered.

"Please take them off."

Pointing to the man in front of him, Ray said, "He didn't have to."

"Sir, please, take them off."

Ray pulled off his shoes for inspection, and the bored man said, "OK, put them on the x-ray conveyer and move through the screening device."

Ray emptied his pockets and took off his belt, and then he felt a soft puff of air hit him as he passed through the device.

"OK, move to your terminal," said the armed TSA agent.

Ray grabbed the basket with his items, walked a few feet, and redressed. After he had finished, he noticed that

Caroline had her hands full of paperwork and, because there was no place to sit down, she had to struggle with her tennis shoes. Ray stepped close to her and grabbed her handbag and the things in her hand. He offered his shoulder to lean on until she had retied her shoes. Ray laughed out loud and said, "Are we having fun yet?"

They found a couple of empty seats in the waiting area and Ray picked up a Field and Stream at the newsstand and read an article about elk hunting in Wyoming. He read a few lines and then showed the page to Caroline, who said nothing but gave him 'that look.'

"I was just thinking that might be another way to earn a few bucks, that's all," he said.

Ray had worn out that magazine by the time they landed in Miami. It was dark by the time they got through the baggage claim. They hailed a taxi and headed for the four-star hotel they had booked for the night. The driver turned down the salsa music long enough to receive directions from Ray. He then cranked it back up and zigzagged through traffic, narrowly missing a bicycle and another cab. The ride in the grimy cab gave Ray the creeps. He was glad to pay the driver fifty bucks just to get out of it.

The hotel was nice. The staff was helpful and got them settled into their room quickly. They were quick to help them but slow to leave; after Ray handed the pair a five apiece, they said thank you and closed the door. Ray and Caroline took a fast shower and moved downstairs to the 24-hour coffee shop. They each enjoyed a piece of apple pie and a cup of decaf to tide them over until breakfast.

As she turned out the light, she said, "Tomorrow night, we'll be sleeping at sea."

"Yeah," said Ray, "and the last time I did that, I was recovering from a bullet wound."

"Yes, I remember getting that call from your mother. Thank God you won't have to do that again. Good night."

"Good night."

The taxi dropped them off in the restricted zone just outside the fenced-off pier. Ray paid the driver and picked up a pair of well filled suitcases. There were a few people waiting at the gate, and Ray and Caroline took their place in line. As they made their way to the front, a pair of smiling young women took their tickets and wrote the cabin number P380 on a pair of luggage tags and fastened them on to the handles. Ray thought of his little Colt back in the hotel safe and said a little prayer for a good time and calm seas. The porters then loaded the suitcases onto a motorized cart to be driven aboard the ship and later delivered to the correct suite. Caroline received a brochure that outlined all of the activities that were available while they were at sea and an itinerary of their ports of call.

They stepped onto the gangplank and walked towards the ship. With every step, the ocean liner kept getting bigger and higher as they closed in on the deck. After reaching the rail, they were greeted by some of the ship's officers dressed in their brilliant white uniforms. The sight was impressive.

"Permission to come aboard," spoke Ray with a smile.

"Permission granted, sailor," said a well-groomed officer with two gold stripes on his sleeve.

Ray fired back, "Marine," and kept walking. They strolled around the main deck for about a half hour watching more people arrive and getting the general layout of the ship. As they walked towards their cabin to see if their baggage had arrived, they detoured long enough to make their way to the main deck in time to see the two smiling young ticket takers lock the gate and step up the ramp to the ship's main deck. Shortly thereafter, the big engines started up and the boatswain mates cast the heavy lines down to the pier below. Caroline squeezed Ray's hand as they watched Miami disappear in the distance.

They settled on an informal dinner for the first evening at the outdoor tiki bar. Each had a simple patty melt and Red Stripe beer for their meal. It was both interesting and fun to watch the parade of overdressed tourists heading for the main dining room, hell bent on eating themselves into the infirmary in the first eight hours of their seven-day vacation.

Ray glanced at the agenda and noticed a small open-air show venue that featured a guitar playing duo that did easy music riffs coupled with a comedy routine.

"Let's go here and check these guys out," he said.

"Fine," said Caroline. "They kind of look like the Smothers Brothers."

"Yeah they do, only younger," said Ray. They spent the remainder of the evening watching the show and downing a few more Red Stripes.

As they made their way back to their cabin, Caroline observed, "Did you see the moon?"

"Yes, I believe that's what's called a lovers moon."

"Pace yourself, Ray, remember it's a seven-day cruise."

Ray laughed and said, "Leave the light on darlin.'" He referred to a Robert Earl Keen song they both knew very well.

They bought hats and t-shirts on Saint Maarten Island, swam with the dolphins off the shore of Saint Lucia, flew in the parasail near Nassau, and in general had a great time on their seven-day voyage.

On their journey back to Miami, Caroline took Ray's hand and told him that she was experiencing some back and shoulder pain. She had not been able to sleep well for a couple of nights and asked Ray to massage her neck. As he laid his hands on her shoulders, he suggested that she may want to see the ship's doctor to get his opinion.

She smiled at Ray and said, "I think I kind of overdid it with that parasail landing. I don't think it is anything serious." Ray continued to massage her back and told her that he would look into some pain medication for her when he was finished. Caroline smiled at Ray and laid a wet washcloth over her eyes. She thanked him for his attention. She rolled on to her bunk and tried catch forty winks.

Although Ray didn't advertise his concern, he knew it was not like Caroline to complain, so he figured the pain was more severe than she had let on. He left the cabin and went to the infirmary to speak with the ship's doctor.

"My wife is not feeling too good, doc. She has a good deal of upper body soreness and is having trouble sleeping."

"Why don't we take a look," the doctor said as he picked up an orange tackle box full of medical supplies and a portable EKG machine. "Lead the way."

Caroline was sitting up when they came through the door, and she didn't object that Ray had slipped out and summoned the ship's doctor. The doctor grabbed his stethoscope and asked her to take a few deep breaths as he moved the microphone around her upper body. He fastened the portable EKG machine to her finger and placed a few probes on her ankles and chest. After the machine spit out a yard of tape, the doctor smiled and turned the machine off.

After removing the probes, he studied the tape and looked into Caroline's eyes.

"It looks like your results are a little bit abnormal. Have you ever had trouble with your heart?"

"No, never," she replied.

"My advice to you is to see your doctor at your earliest opportunity. I don't see anything alarming here, but it doesn't show a perfectly normal pattern, either. I am going to dispense a dozen baby aspirin to you. I think you should take one aspirin after breakfast and one after dinner. I think it would be prudent to avoid stressful situations until you get a more complete checkup. Would you like for me to call the port and have emergency services take a look at you when we dock in a few hours?"

"No thank you, doctor, I feel pretty good right now and I feel better today than I did yesterday, so I don't believe I'll need it. I do promise to see my doctor as soon as I get home."

"OK then. If you have any concerns, please call me. I hope that you folks had a great vacation."

"Yes we did, doctor, thank you."

As they headed for shore, they found a quiet spot on deck and relaxed in a couple of deck chairs. Caroline put her discomfort on hold and tried to keep the conversation light. She took note that Ray had almost blended in his farmer's tan and remarked about what a good and completely irresponsible time they had enjoyed. Ray nodded and began to confide that for as long as he could remember, he had always carried the heavy weight of responsibility. First, it was taking care of the basic necessities of his family, and then later it grew to provide for the salaries and welfare of his employees. When he became prosperous and had the financial ability to live a life of leisure, he chose to take on the care and feeding of his livestock and his land, which could be a 24-hour-a-day job.

"I guess it is woven into my fabric," he said. "I just can't understand how people can get up in the morning and have nothing to do but play games. It seems like such a waste to be just a consumer. I enjoy creating, making things, and caring for things. A man has just so many days to live and sitting in a swimming pool drinking beer seems like such a wasteful use of that time when you think about it."

As the big motors droned towards Miami, Ray mused that this time at sea had reminded him of the week he spent on the hospital ship Mercy off the coast of Viet Nam. After a week of being horizontal, he was able to walk, supported with a cane, and was allowed to gather his gear and transfer stateside. He was then transported to a Navy air base near San Francisco for his discharge from active duty and the start of his new life with Caroline.

"This trip has given us a chance to relax both physically and mentally," he continued. "I want you to know that I am grateful every day that I wake up next to you and that we enjoy the life that we live. If you take the time to look away from the tourist venues, it gives you a perspective of what life is like for others in this world. My time in Viet Nam gave me that perspective when I was young. I didn't want that kind of life in the United States, especially for the boys." As the haze from the city began to appear on the horizon, Ray looked at

Caroline and admitted that he had truly enjoyed their time together and was happy that they had this time to themselves.

Little did they know that within twenty-four hours, their lives would be changed forever. A series of seemingly inconsequential events formed the perfect storm, a storm that altered their ideal lives in a way that was good for no one.

Chapter 10

The Incident

Ray's eyes opened to the sound of a vending machine dropping an aluminum can down the chute. He was awake now and began to take stock of his surroundings. Caroline was still sleeping; she looked more tan than usual and very relaxed. The vacation, it seemed, was good for her. He lay motionless for a while, trying not to wake her. He used this time to reflect on the previous week and to plan the remainder of the day.

Ray had to admit that he had enjoyed the cruise, but he missed his ranch and the inner peace that it gave him. He had also endured enough humidity to last a lifetime. One more day and he would be winging his way back to Wyoming and its crisp, dry mornings.

As Ray got up and made his way to the coffee maker, Caroline opened her eyes.

She asked, as she stretched, "What do you have in mind for today?"

"Ah, just killin' time 'till we can head back to the ranch," he said. "I sure miss Wyoming. I plan on cooling my jets in the pool this morning but after that, I have nothing in mind except to retrieve my old Colt from the hotel safe."

"It will be good to get home and get busy again. This Miami, well, it's one hellava hot and uncomfortable place to be." Caroline said, "There is a theater located a few blocks away. Why don't we catch a movie during the hot part of the day? That should eat up a good portion of the afternoon today, and tomorrow we can spend the morning packing and getting to the airport."

"Sure, Carol, that's as good a plan as any," Ray agreed. "I have heard enough of the noisy ice machine and the midnight drunks to last me a lifetime. Sounds like a winner to me and it's close enough to walk."

Ray climbed out of the pool around noon and bought a burger and a Miller Lite for himself and a burger and a diet cola for Caroline. They sat under a large umbrella and talked about their options at the multiplex theatre. After they finished eating, they went upstairs to shower off the pool residue and dress for the movie.

Ray showered first and put on his comfortable shorts and a pair of camouflage styled Crocs. Before he put on his Hawaiian shirt, he grabbed his old Colt pistol, racked in a round, locked the safety, and topped off the magazine. He then tucked the sleek little Colt 1903 into a holster on the inside of his waistband. As Caroline showered, Ray recalled fond memories of his old Colt.

Ray's father had mailed the little gun to Ray in 1966 while Ray was in Viet Nam. Ray had carried it almost every day of his nine month and twenty-one day tour of duty. He recalled that once, when he was separated from his squad and his rifle, the little Colt was used to counter enemy fire while he was running back to cover. He also remembered how the little gun had kept him and a friend from being attacked by a gang of locals when he was off-duty in Saigon. The old Colt had been relegated to the gun safe at home and probably hadn't been fired in forty years. The little .32 caliber wasn't really a very practical gun for Wyoming; it was far too weak of a round to be effective against any of the natural predators found in those parts. The little .32 had just one use: it was made to be concealed and used to discourage soft-bodied predators from attacking good people.

Caroline put on a pair of white shorts and a pink blouse and matching pink sandals.

"The show will start in less than an hour; we had better get downstairs if we don't want to be late," she said.

"OK, OK. I have the room key and my wallet. Let's go."

There was a good deal of pedestrian traffic once they left the hotel. Ray and Caroline fell behind some Haitian women who were apparently just getting off work from one of the hotels. They all stopped at a traffic light and exchanged smiles and nods. When the light turned to green, they began to cross the avenue, some in front and some behind Ray and Caroline. As they reached the center of the intersection, an emerald green Hummer H2 with blacked-out windows moved close to the crosswalk and, just as Caroline passed in front, the driver blasted a train whistle loud enough to break glass.

Caroline jumped back, startled from the obscene blast of noise. She stumbled and grabbed for Ray's arm as she fell to her knees. Ray held her up and he looked directly into her eyes. Ray had seen those eyes for more than forty years, forty years that had changed her hair to a salt-and-pepper grey and her outward look to a more mature woman. Her eyes always had that spark of optimism, of peace, of happiness. It was a spark that had never changed … until that moment.

Two Haitian ladies began to help Ray support her body, and one woman began to express her outrage to the driver of the Hummer, who rolled down his window to spew a few obscenities back to her. As they laid Caroline down on the asphalt, Ray saw the fear in her eyes, and then she was gone. Her spark, her pulse, and her life had disappeared.

He tried to understand what had happened. He was confused. *Weren't we just going to the movies?* He wondered. *Why is she dead? Oh my God. She is dead!*

It was at that moment that Ray heard a call of, "Hey, hey, hey!" that rang out from the Hummer. The driver's window was down and Rondell "doom" Macdume smiled at him, exposing his gold grille and laughing with one of the others in the car.

Ray overheard one of the Hummer's back-seat passengers ask, "Did you see dat lilly bitch jump when you hit da whistle?"

Rondell replied with a smile, "Yeah, that's what I'm talking about. Ha ha!" By then the traffic light had changed and Rondell blew the train whistle again and again saying, "Get your bitch out of my way, I have places to be. Move your white ass now or I'll crush both of you like the crackers you are!" Ray knelt on the hot asphalt, trying his best to revive his wife, but the violent noise and harassment caused his mind to flash back to his last day of combat in Viet Nam.

"I'm hit! I'm hit, Ray, help me!"

"OK Ace, I'm coming!"

I have to get to him. I'll leave my rifle and get him. Gotta go. Right now while the boys have them occupied. Just a few more steps and I'll be there! God, he looks scared.

"Ace, can you get up? Let me help you to my shoulder. Come on man, let's go."

God he is heavy, now we are taking fire. I can make it, almost there, damn, I'm hit too. Gotta make it another ten feet, gotta make ..."

Ray felt a surge of adrenaline shake his body. The hair stood up on his neck and he felt flushed, with his body heat reaching the boiling point. He struggled to free his arm from under Caroline's head and, while still on his knees, turned to face the men in the Hummer. The grin had not gone from the driver's face as Ray reached under his shirt and then, in that instant, Ray's mind slipped into a place that was exiled deep inside, a place he had tamped down and spent his life trying to quiet but try as he might, he could not control the demons that surfaced when primal emotions came calling. Time stood still.

Ray's subconscious brain took control of his body. The view through his eyes was like a moving picture; his hands and arms moved without will. It suddenly seemed as though everything that was happening was clear, effortless, and precise. Like his younger days in Viet Nam, his senses were absolutely acute.

The old Colt seemed to be an extension of his arm. It came up, with the tiny sight looking as large as a telephone pole. Suddenly, a red dot appeared on the forehead of the driver as the muffled sound of the pistol echoed in the acrid air. The driver's head jerked backward, and then his body slumped over the console. Next, Ray saw the front passenger open the door and stand up on the running board. Red flashes and lead came from a chrome revolver fired wildly across the roof.

Ray took two shots through the open driver's window, hitting the passenger in the stomach. He could hear the revolver hit the car and then the pavement as the man followed it to the ground. The rear window began to open. Ray fired two rounds into the lowering glass. As it stopped, the fourth passenger opened the offside door, grabbed the fallen pistol and, using the car as cover, ran towards the crowd that was forming at the opposite corner.

As the sirens were approaching, Ray holstered his gun. He turned his undivided attention to his wife and began to weep. The Haitian women and the bystanders all disappeared when the police started to close in.

Ray was in handcuffs as the Emergency Medical Team declared his wife deceased. They placed her body on a stretcher and rolled it over to the emergency medical vehicle and shortly thereafter left the scene.

Ray retched and beckoned the officer to stand aside so he could relieve his churning stomach. He was sick, bewildered, and empty inside. After he had regained control of his emotions, he sat quietly as his rights were read to him in the back of the patrol car. His old Colt lay next to its half-empty magazine on the hood of the cruiser.

CHAPTER 11

THE RIDE

"I know what we said about your Miranda rights at the scene," said the policeman in the passenger seat, "but I just want to tell you that you did us and the city of Miami a big favor back there."

"Don't ask me to repeat that outside this car, but those three punks have been in and out of jail so many times it's sickening," said the officer driving the cruiser.

"People like that have nothing to lose, so nothing ever gets to them. They just keep coming back again and again. They know the system and they work it to their advantage. They don't care if they are put into the jail; they just consider it part of the cost of doing business," the policeman continued. "Nevertheless, I think you are going to be in some deep shit when this story hits the networks. You know that Rondell had a gun, but it was still in his console. The other two you shot were unarmed. My name is George La Monica, and I'll help you all I can, but I have to level with you, man. This is going to be a hot issue for a while."

Without looking up, Ray spoke, "Right now I don't give a damn about my Miranda rights. I don't care whether they live or die, or even if I live or die. I just don't care. Those four assholes stalked us, they picked out my wife as a victim, and they nailed us without any warning. I believe it was simply because we were the only white people in the crosswalk. To be honest, I'm glad I shot them."

"I didn't hear that. Did you, Bob?'

"Hear what?" answered the passenger.

"What was that bit about four of them? There were four of them and you let one get away?" asked George.

"Yeah, I guess I did. He must have taken the chrome revolver with him when he left. The guy with the shots to the gut fired it at me three times."

"You mean the survivor?" asked Bob.

"The others died?" Ray asked.

"Yes, I thought you knew," said George.

"No I didn't. Frankly, I didn't think that gun had the power to kill a man even from that distance. Especially through the glass."

"A shot to the forehead and a shot to the temple will do it almost every time. We found no evidence that anyone shot a gun except you," George said. "Nobody interviewed said anything about return fire. Without the fourth guy, the gun, or a witness, you are up the proverbial creek."

Ray pondered what had just happened. His wife was gone, and his life as he knew it was likely over. He was beginning a plummet down to hell on earth. The remainder of his ride was pretty quiet as he mentally tried to find the words to tell his son of the terrible event that had just taken place.

They entered the sally port and the two officers put on their cop faces and opened the back door. They guided Ray into the induction area, where Ray was fingerprinted, photographed, and booked into the system.

George said, "The detectives will interview you now. Just tell them the truth and don't leave anything out; you will need every bit of help you can get. They will let you make a short telephone call when they are done. I know the homicide detectives feel pretty much like I do about this bunch, but don't expect them to cut you a break. There is too much outside and inside pressure on the department to burn you," George said as he gestured to the picture of the black police chief on the wall.

Chapter 12

Seeking Justice

"Danny, this is Dad," Ray said into the phone.

"Hey, world traveler! Are you guys ready for the plane ride home tomorrow?"

"I am afraid not, Danny. I have to tell you some bad news." Danny could tell by his father's tone that there was big trouble on the other end of the line. "Danny, some things have happened and your mother has had a heart attack and she … well, she has died," Ray said quietly.

"What? That can't be! No … No … No!"

"Danny, there is more. I have been arrested and put in jail here in Miami and I'm in a real tight spot. You will soon be hearing all about it on the news. I am being charged with murder. There is this attorney named Ken Allen who works at the public defender's office that has been given my case, and he is the only soul I can talk to down here. I have half the people in the jail trying to kill me."

"What the hell did you do?" Danny asked.

"I shot some punks that scared your mother to death." The detective pointed at his wrist watch to remind Ray to end the call and he responded by telling Danny, "They have only given me a few minutes on this call so I can't tell you the whole story right now, but when you see the news, don't believe what they say, at least the part about me being a bad guy."

"We'll get down to Miami and help you out as soon as we can!"

"No, Danny, just take care of the place with Hector. There isn't anything that you can do down here except to get your mother's body returned back to Wyoming. She is being held at the county coroner's office. Please just take care of her. I'll be all right. They have me in solitary right now until things simmer down. Goodbye, son, be strong." There was a click as Ray ended the call.

"What is going on?" asked Jan.

"I'm not sure of exactly what has happened, but apparently Mom has had a heart attack and passed away."

"Oh my God," she said.

"Dad also said that he was in jail and was being charged with murder." Jan looked like she was ready to vomit; she held her stomach and bowed her head as if she were avoiding the reality of her husband's words. "This is just awful. It couldn't get any worse," Danny said. "Dad said to watch the news and he said not to believe what we hear."

"Oh Lord!" Jan said. "Call your brother and tell him what your dad said. I'll go to Hector's house and let him know while you're on the phone."

Later that evening, they tuned into the national news and heard the following bulletin:

Earlier today, there was another racial shooting in Florida. An elderly man from Wyoming who was visiting on vacation shot at a car filled with unarmed black teens, killing two and severely injuring a third occupant.

"Do you know what set off the incident?" the news anchor asked the reporter from Florida.

"From what we gather, the teens pranked him by blowing their horn at him while he was crossing the street and he took it upon himself to shoot at them." The reporter shook his head and looked directly at the camera, then said, "When will this sort of thing ever end? There are simply too many guns on the street and too many intemperate people carrying them. Community leaders are asking for calm. Services for the murdered teens will

be conducted at Mt. Olive Baptist Church on Saturday, and Reverend Camsson D. Meek with several other dignitaries will do the eulogy. And now on to other news ..."

"I guess that says it all. When he said he was in a fix, I guess he meant it!"

Jan looked up with a fearful, sad expression and said, "Danny, it occurs to me that you may never see your dad again as a free man! I have got to do something. I am going down there to help with his defense. That is the least I can do."

"Let's talk in the morning," Danny said. "We have so much to think about, so much to do."

The next day, Danny and Jan contacted the authorities in Miami. The conversation went something like this:

"Coroner's office."

"Yes, my name is Danny Jordan. I received a telephone call last night that informed me that my mother had passed away yesterday."

"You say Jordan? Oh yes, Caroline Jordan, heart attack. She came in yesterday around two in the afternoon."

"What do I have to do to have her body sent back to our home here in Wyoming for burial?"

"Well, normally the air carriers can have the body shipped back once it goes to the mortician, but your mother's body has been put on a legal hold because it may be needed to be used as evidence in a murder case."

"Answer me this, my friend. How does a heart attack figure into a murder case? I just don't get it." Danny said.

"Well, the lady, your mother, died because of the train whistle horn on the kid's car."

"Now it's starting to make sense. So you are saying she has to stay there?"

"Yes, that's what I'm saying. She will stay here until the trial is over or the state prosecutor says to release her. You can give them a try; the prosecutor of this case is named Frances James. I am sorry, sir, but I can't help you any more." Click.

Danny felt beaten. He reached for his laptop and searched for the prosecutor's office information. Shortly thereafter, he dialed the number.

"State Attorney's office."

"Yes, my name is Danny Jordan and I understand that your office is prosecuting my father on a murder case."

"Oh yes, we are."

"Is it possible for me to speak with Frances James?"

"I'm afraid not, sir. We do not converse with anyone from the defendant's side unless it is in public or in depositions."

"I'm not interested in talking about my father's case. I simply want to get my mother's body laid to rest here in Wyoming."

"All I can tell you is to put your request in writing and mail it to Prosecutor James and we will take it from there. That is all I can do for you right now. Goodbye, sir."

Danny felt like he had been punched in the gut again.

Jan put her hand on his shoulder and said, "I'll get down there and do what I can to get these kinds of things done. Danny, I have to go. If I was a seamstress or a secretary, I would stay here with you, but I am a lawyer and I am part of this family. It is my duty to go." Danny reluctantly nodded his head in agreement.

"Take Hector and get yourself settled in a safe place. After you are secure, Hector can return. I will stay here as Dad requested and take care of the kids and the homestead. Please be careful. I am sure these guys have some pretty bad friends and there may be people out there looking to exact some kind of revenge. You would likely be an easy target. Jan, why don't you consider using your maiden name?"

Jan smiled warmly and replied, "Jordan is pretty common. I don't think it will be necessary, but I will consider it once I see what I have to deal with."

"No Jan, I insist that you use Armstrong while you are gone. I don't want you getting hurt."

"Sure enough, I'll do it for you."

Danny turned his efforts into finding transportation for Jan and Hector. He was able to book two seats on a red-eye that was leaving in just a few hours. They landed in Miami, secured a rental car, and made their way to the jail before noon the next day.

"What the heck are you doing here?" said Ray through the button-activated speaker on the other side of the glass. His eyes got teary as he saw his lawyer Ken Allen flanked by Jan and Hector.

Reaching down to press the button for the speaker, Hector said, "I came out to help Jan get settled. She is going to work with Ken and get you out of here."

"I have my doubts, Hector," Ray said. "I saw the news tonight and all the major media has me pegged as an old man that can't take a joke from some innocent teenagers. Not a single word about Caroline. Not a damn word about the long rap sheet on the felons in the car whose average age was twenty-two. All they talk about is that I am just a cranky old man with a gun who didn't like black teenagers. It is all a bunch of crap! I'm being set up by the damn propagandists. I'll take my lumps. I did it sure enough but by God, why can't they tell the truth about what happened? Why does everything have to be so damn one-sided?"

Ray shook his head and tried to compose himself. He cracked a small smile and looked at the trio on the other side of the glass.

Hector pressed the talk button and informed Ray that his ranch was being well cared for by saying, "A couple of your neighbors have sent over one of their hands to help your son run the ranch until I return. I am sure that they will keep things running smoothly for a couple more days."

Ray replied, "That was damn nice of them."

"It was," followed Hector, "but everyone is pretty sick about what has happened to you and they are all pitching in to help us until things return to normal. They all figure, that if the roles were reversed and they were in a tight spot, that you would step up and help them if they needed it."

"I like to think that I would. Listen, I know this cop. His name is George La Monica. He works the day shift here at the station. He was the guy that took me into custody after the shooting. I think the guy has his heart in the right place and he kind of offered to help me if he could do it in a quiet way. Have Jan check with him when you leave here. Maybe he can point you in the right direction for a safe place for Jan."

While Ken sat down with Jan and Ray to bring him up to speed on the case, Hector moved over a few panels to a Mexican woman with a small child who was speaking to her husband through the glass. Hector respectfully waited until she acknowledged his presence by turning and looking directly at him. Hector nodded a thank you and began to speak to the inmate:

Disculpa puedo hablar con tu esposo? Grasias, miraste a este hombre aya? El es mi major amigo el me dio un buen trabajo cuando nadie me quiso dar. Yo estoy seguro que los negros ban a tartar de agarrarlo. El es una buen muchacho no pertenece a este lugar. Por favor pasa esta palabra al rededor tu yo es un buen muchacho yo estoy tratando de ayudarlo a salir de este lugar. Grasias.

This meant: "Pardon me. May I speak to your husband? Thank you. Do you see this guy over there? He is my best friend and he gave me a good job when nobody else would. I am sure the blacks will be out to get him. He is a good guy and he doesn't belong in this place. Please pass the word around that he is an honorable man and try and help him out if you can. Thank you." The hard Mexican looked up at Hector and nodded.

As Jan and Hector left the jail complex, they walked around the corner into the front lobby of the police station and approached the clerk at the front counter. Jan smiled and asked, "Would it be possible to speak with officer George La Monica?"

"He's on duty right now, but if you like, you may leave a message for him to call you. I am not at liberty to give you his phone number."

"That would be great."

"Write your name and phone number on this paper and I'll see to it that he gets it before the end of his shift."

"Thanks, I appreciate your help," Jan said.

On the way back to her motel from the jail, Jan's phone rang.

"Hey, this is George, do I know you?"

"Not yet," was Jan's cheerful reply. "I am Ray Jordan's daughter-in-law and I hope to work on his case. Ray said that you volunteered to help if you could."

"Yeah, I said that. So what is it that you need?"

"I need a safe place to stay, a place that is kind of off the beaten path, a place where I can work without being hounded by the media."

George cleared his throat and said, "Let me check on a few things. I'll call you back around six o'clock tonight."

"That would be great. I'll be waiting to hear from you, and thank you."

At 5:40 p.m., Jan's phone rang again.

"This is George. I have a place where you can stay."

"Really? That quick? Where is it and when can I see it?" Jan asked.

"Well I spoke to my wife Debbie and explained the situation, and she has agreed to let you use our guest room for the duration of the trial. We also have our daughter's room, which, now since she is in college, is almost never used. We are less than fifteen minutes from the courthouse, so it should be very convenient for you. My wife can always use someone nice to talk to when I have the night shift."

Jan asked, "Do you mind if we come over now?"

"Well, we will be eating in about 45 minutes, but any time after 7:30 would be fine."

"Then 7:30 it is. I look forward to meeting you and Debbie. Oh, I need your address so that I can program it into the global positioning system in the rental car."

"It's 3006 Lemay Street."

"Got it, see you soon, and thanks."

They drove up to a neat home in a tidy subdivision and pulled directly into the driveway. Next to the perfectly manicured lawn, there was a twenty-foot Grady White boat with a Bimini top and twin black max outboard motors centered on a cement pad located next to the garage. There were two BMW motorcycles inside one of the three open garage doors.

George came out of the house and greeted the pair.

Hector extended his right hand and said, "I am Hector. I work with Mr. Jordan. And this is his daughter-in-law, Jan Armstrong."

"Welcome," George said. "Let's get into the air conditioning. I am about to melt out here."

After Jan was introduced to Debbie, they began to discuss Ray's predicament.

"I know that you are going to have your hands full on this case. Will you actually be doing the defense?" Debbie asked.

"No. I am a lawyer, but I am expecting to be more of an assistant and a counselor to Ray. I have no legal status in Florida at this time. I'm just trying to help out any way that I can."

"Would you like to move in soon?"

"Yes, I'd like to get settled in as quickly as possible. Hector has a lot of work stacking up at the ranch and I can't wait to get this trial over with. George, I know that there are some potential problems that may arise and I want you to know, should you feel any heat from your department, I will move away as quickly as I came in."

George replied, "I believe that Ray is a good man and this is a righteous case; otherwise I wouldn't have offered to help you. If we get a little heat, well, so be it. I have twenty-four years in now. I can pull the plug and get my retirement any time I want."

"Well, thanks for the vote of confidence. I insist on paying you, so how much?"

"I hadn't expected any payment. I didn't do this to make money," said George.

"Well, thanks and all that, but it costs money to keep that Grady White full of fuel. How about $2,000 per month for the bedroom, bath, and access to the second bedroom as an office? Listen, if you don't take it, the lawyers and experts we have to pay will get it all."

"OK, but just remember, you don't have to pay me."

"Fine, here is your payment," Jan said, handing Debbie a check from her checkbook. "I'll come back in the morning. Thank you both so much. It will feel good to be in such a beautiful home with some nice people."

CHAPTER 13

FINDING EDWARDS

"All rise!" rang through the courtroom.

The judge looked like a big eagle ready to pounce on his prey, with his black robe flailing to the sides and a stern, disapproving look. The bald-headed jurist enjoyed a bit of inner happiness by intimidating all of the green public defenders as he walked into the courtroom. He liked to push, cajole, and confuse those lawyers just out of school or those he considered lazy career bureaucratic fixtures in the public defender's office. He considered any lawyer who was not in private practice to be a gutless example and an embarrassment to the occupation he held in such high esteem.

"Your Honor, we wish to file a motion for bail to be offered to our defendant," said Ken Allen, faking his confidence.

Judge May acted as though nothing had been said and contemptuously studied some papers in front of him. After a short period of disinterest, he looked at Ken Allen and said, "In light of the fact that your client is not a resident of Florida and the very serious nature of the charges filed, your motion is denied. There will be no bail allowed. I would like to expedite this case, counselor. Can you be ready to start trial in 60 days?"

"I believe so, Your Honor."

"You believe so?"

"The answer is yes, Your Honor, we will be ready."

"Good, then. Trial is set for October fourteenth at nine o'clock a.m." With a slap of the gavel, he looked to the bailiff and said, "Next case."

S. L. BENELLI

Two deputies grabbed Ray beneath his arms and lifted him from his seat. Ray wore an orange jumpsuit with his hands cuffed and chained to his shackled feet. Ray nodded at Jan as he was led from the camera-filled courtroom back to his private cell inside the county jail.

Judge Peter May was a big man, well over six foot three and an easy 300 pounds. He had a strictly business personality and flew through cases from the moment he walked into the courtroom until well after the other judges had gone home for the day. He was unusually ethical and ambitious for a liberal and, as a rule he tried to remove himself from any outside influences that were found in and around the courthouse.

But, this case was different. Peter May was, in his heart, a true believer of the beneficence of big government. He was also a supporter of gun control and, while he avoided talking business outside of the courtroom, he often made exceptions whenever he was asked about guns or their use by non-law enforcement citizens. He never passed up the opportunity to speak publicly on the issue. He honestly believed that the police could be relied upon to protect the public, and that guns in private hands were the cause of many of the ills of society. This case, if concluded correctly, could validate his viewpoint with an exclamation point and possibly make his upcoming retirement a great deal more lucrative.

Jan Armstrong, Ray's daughter-in-law, had witnessed the scene in the courtroom. She was not a criminal defense attorney, but she had enough experience in courtrooms to know when someone was being kicked around by the judge. She was keenly aware that Ray's lawyer had been battered and disrespected. She knew instinctively that Ken Allen had waded into the Miami surf to a point way over his head. If Ray was to have any chance of returning to Wyoming, they would need to look for someone who was tough and smart for their counsel. She knew Ken was trying his best and that he had the best of intentions, but he had little chance of prevailing in a courtroom that regarded him so lightly.

She met with Ray after the hearing and they decided to prospect for some better representation. Jan studied the Florida Law Review and determined that there were a few top-notch trial attorneys in the Miami area. She did a few interviews in person and, with Ray's approval, settled on a man named Jack Edwards as their first choice.

Jack Edwards was a man who was well-known throughout the southern United States. He wore a tan suede suit coat with a western-style yoke and a string tie that had a turquoise stone as an accent. He usually wore a pair of Lucchese boots made from ostrich hide and, when he was outside of the courtroom, he could be seen in a high-quality white Stetson ten-gallon hat. He was as thin as a rail and had a bit of facial hair that resembled a turn-of-the-century gunfighter. For his steed, he rode the leather of a new silver Corvette. He was the John Wesley Hardin of Florida. He was also a man who had the reputation of a winner, someone who would do or say whatever was necessary to be victorious. He feared no judge.

"I have read about the case. I like it," said Jack. "If you agree to my terms, I would be glad to represent you."

"And what would those terms be?" Jan inquired.

"I will represent you and provide you with all of the resources of my firm for one million dollars. As you probably know, I don't handle a lot of cases, I only take on cases that I believe in, and I have a very good record of success."

"I know. I have studied your history. We can handle the million dollars and, I can speak for Ray, we want your services. What would be your payment schedule?"

"Judge May works really fast. We will need a lot of help right away, so I would like half of the money now and the other half when the trial begins."

"Done," Jan said. "Give me a transfer number and we can wire the cash to you tomorrow."

Jack called to his secretary and asked her to take Jan into her adjacent office and to attend to the details of the money transfer.

In Jan's absence, Jack picked up the telephone and asked for the State Attorney; after a minute, he said, "Yes, my name is Jack Edwards." There was a short pause and then you could hear him say, "Hello, Jimmy. Yes, fine, fine. I have taken on this Ray Jordan case. Yes … of course. We sure don't want to see our client in shackles and cuffs again, great! I'll see to it that he has a nice looking suit to match mine. OK, OK. It will be a regular suit, how's that? Thanks … You too … See you in court," Jack said as he laughed.

In one minute, Jack had begun to change the direction of the trial. The state had been put on notice that they were not going to abuse Ray Jordan any more.

Jan overheard the conversation and said, "Thank you sir, it made me sick to see him being led around like he was some kind of animal. Jack, I know that you are aware that I am Ray's daughter-in-law, but I am also a licensed attorney from the State of Nebraska. I would like to offer my assistance to you in any way you find appropriate."

Jack quickly asked, "Have you been granted a waiver to practice in Florida?"

"I have submitted a request, but it is being held up in Tallahassee."

Jack answered, "Don't plan on having any progress on that issue soon enough to impact this trial. Jan, I don't want to hurt your feelings, but frankly, I think it would be better for everyone if you weren't connected with my firm. It could become a sideshow and a distraction from our main goal, which is to get Ray out of jail and back to Wyoming. I have an idea. Let me work on it for you. In the meantime, stay in touch and continue informing Ray on what is going on."

"Thanks."

"By the way, who is representing Ray now?"

"Ken Allen at the public defender's office."

"I'll call him and have him send over all of the files to me."

"I'll also call him. I need to thank him for the work he has done."

Later that day, Jan called Ken Allen to inform him of the changes she had made.

"Ken, this is Jan Armstrong. I wanted to call you and thank you for the help that you have given to Ray and me."

"Well, it has been my pleasure to serve you," he said.

"Ken, we have hired Jack Edwards as our lead attorney on this case, and I wanted to tell you personally and let you know how much we appreciated your help when Ray needed it the most."

Ken replied, "I'm sorry that I can't help you more, but I am happy to have met you."

"Ken, would you please see to it that all of the files and information you have on this case be given to Edwards and Bloodworth?"

"Yes ma'am, I will bring it over personally if I can. You know that they must submit a request for the information."

"I do know and his office is planning on calling you later today. Thanks again, Ken."

The following day, Jan's phone rang. On the other end was a woman named Sondra Dale. Sondra and her partner, Anne Hill, owned a company known as Hill and Dale Consulting Service, a small firm of jury consultants that Jack Edwards used to help him select the most favorable jurors. They were one of the reasons that Jack had been so successful in the past. They gave Jack an unseen edge that only the elite trial attorneys used to increase their advantage.

"Jack called me this morning and told me of your predicament. He said you would like to work closely on this trial, but not in an official capacity. You'll need courtroom access and an ability to speak with Jack without being part of the legal team or identified as family. He says that you have some legal background."

"Yes, I am a law professor and a licensed lawyer in Nebraska."

"Can we meet for lunch today?" Sondra asked.

"Sure. I am going to the courthouse around eleven to talk to Ray. I can meet you at a restaurant nearby."

Sondra said, "There is a small Cuban sandwich shop across the street; I'll see you there at 12:30. I'll be wearing a green pant suit."

"I look forward to meeting with you," said Jan.

Jan sat at an outside table and noticed a Lincoln Town Car drive into the lot behind the restaurant. She saw a small woman emerge from the tan leather seat wearing a green pant suit. She stood up and extended her hand as the woman came near.

"My name is Jan Armstrong, are you?"

"Sondra Dale," she interrupted with a smile.

"Please sit down. Can I get you anything?"

"I am a little hungry. Why don't we split a pressed Cuban?" Sondra suggested.

"Good idea." They gave the waiter the order and began to talk.

"Sondra, I would like to help out on this case as much as I can. I have secured a safe place to live and I really want to get this nightmare over with and get back home to my family."

"Jan, I have studied this case and I am pretty sure that Ray is going to need all of the help he can muster to get out of Dade County. I would like you to be a part of that team. Jack called me and told me of your request and this is what I can do. I will hire you at the average salary of my associates and I will assign you, with my hands-on assistance, solely to this case."

"It isn't necessary to put me on the payroll," Jan said.

"Yes it is. Everything will be above board. You will be my employee. You will dress the part and work closely with me on this trial. I also think it is a good idea to keep your relationship with Ray quiet."

"I agree. That's why I am using my maiden name."

"Yes. That was very smart. We want you to be alive so you can return to Wyoming when we are done. Do you have a gun?" Sondra asked.

"No. I didn't think it was a good idea to bring one, under the circumstances."

"Well, I have one," she said as she patted her purse, "and my Walther is almost always with me. Nevertheless, we don't want to use it, so don't blow your cover."

The two diminutive ladies made small talk over their sandwich. When they finished eating, Sondra handed Jan her business card and told her to be at the office the next day at 9 a.m.

Jan smiled and said, "Yes, ma'am."

The following day, Jan pulled her car into a space behind a nondescript building in a quiet office complex. There was a bicycle shop, a small diner, and a chiropractic office within sight as she shut off the key. She noticed that the Hill and Dale building was small and had mirror-like reflective glass in the windows. Two infrared cameras were located under the eaves at the corners of the building.

"Good morning Jan, come on in," Sondra said. "This is my partner, Anne Hill." Anne was an elderly woman with an easygoing personality. She greeted Jan with a strong Georgia accent and a pleasant smile. "Anne is the brains of the operation," Sondra said. "She is the one who mainly digs up the information on our prospective jurors."

The office was rather plain, as low-cut carpet and painted trim were the norm. There was a conference room, a large computer room, an office for Anne and an office for Sondra. There was a centrally located break room, where Sondra gestured to Jan to sit down.

"Would you like a cup of coffee?"

"Yes please, just a touch of milk. Thank you."

After Sondra delivered the cup to Jan, she filled one for herself and sat down. She took a sip and got a faraway look in her eye.

Sondra spoke slowly and quietly. "Jan, let me explain what we do here. That room is our computer room. We have the latest in data mining software. It has the capacity to find and store data on almost everyone in Dade County. We can locate things in here that many of these people don't want anyone to know about. We have the ability to gather information on every potential juror in this county. Four weeks before the trial, the jury summonses are mailed out. We start compiling information on those people who are potential jurors. After we get the rough information on these people, we rate them and note anything that may be of interest to Jack. Anne and I have a practical background in psychology and in sociology so we try to weed out the zealots if we can, at least the zealots that would be against us. It is amazing what people will tell you about themselves on Twitter and Facebook. The perfect jury would be one that was made up of one dominant personality sympathetic to our client and several dunces that would follow him or her. It doesn't happen that way very often, but we do our best to make it happen when we can. I like to think that we are a sort of civilian version of the CIA, or the NSA might be more appropriate these days. We have the ability to know if someone has been in the hospital or jail and for what, if they are married or divorced and why. We know if you subscribe to certain magazines, have a membership to clubs or organizations, if you are liberal or conservative, how much money you have, and where that money is kept. We know what kind of car you drive, where you live, and on and on. I think you get it. Just for demonstration purposes, I'll have Anne run your name. Anne, its Janice Jordan Nebraska."

Within seconds, information started to arrive. "College Graduate, JD Degree as Janice Armstrong. Married, two children, born March 5th 1971, parents in Waltham, Mass. In-laws in Wyoming. Played baseball, registered Republican, owns a home with a taxable value of $166,000, has an IRA worth $141,000 and a joint bank account with $19,000 in checking. Employed as a college professor at NSC Chadron, and you subscribe to three magazines: Home and Garden, Equus, and Horse and Rider."

"So Jan, if you didn't know Ray and you were in the jury pool, would you pick yourself to be on his jury?" Sondra asked.

"Sure, I could see his side for sure," Jan said.

"On a scale from one to ten, where would you put yourself?"

"I'd be a nine."

"Well, I'd put you at five or maybe six."

"Why?"

"Because from what I see, you are a law and order person. Because you are a lawyer, you may have seen some guilty people get away with things that you might be sore about. Not only that, you are the kind of person who takes orders from authority figures and almost always complies with their wishes even if you don't like what they are saying. I like the fact that you are conservative, that's a plus, but what bothers me is your law background. People who work in the university system and in the legal profession tend to follow directions very well. It occurs to me that you may have a greater than average inclination to follow the judge's instructions to the letter, and if he dictates his instructions in such a narrow way as to limit the options to guilty or guiltier, you will be stuck. What I'm looking for is the juror who will tell the judge to go to hell and deliver a just verdict."

"So you want a jury nullifier?" Jan asked.

"Not exactly. We just want people who think and act in a sensible, rational way, people who can cut through the chaff and understand the big picture."

Now, Jan had the faraway look in her eye as the words that were spoken began to sink in.

CHAPTER 14

CUTTING THE FIELD

Jack Edwards answered the ringing phone by saying, "Law office."

"Hello Jack, I have some bad news for you about the jury pool," Sondra said. "The names have just been released for the month of October and they look heavily skewed with minorities."

Jack wondered out loud and responded, "I think that you should do a little more research, and then we can meet face to face and go over what you have found."

"OK, we'll continue to work on this data for the remainder of today and tomorrow. We should be able to nail down all of the statistics for you by Wednesday. Where and when would you like to meet?"

Jack looked at his calendar and responded, "How about Wednesday morning at your place?"

"OK, we'll see you at ten o'clock Wednesday morning, here. Bye, Jack." Sondra returned the phone to the cradle.

Anne came into the room with the roster of jurors and laid it down in front of Sondra and Jan. She looked directly at Jan and said, "Preliminary data shows 41% black jurors, 36% Cuban / Hispanic jurors, 21% white jurors, and 2% other. 72% Democrats, 24% Republicans, 2% Libertarians and 2% all others combined."

"This is not good news for Ray. We better get busy and find some anomalies in here that will help our side," said Sondra.

Anne moved into the computer room and began to download files on each of the 375 potential jurors. She soon burned up about three reams of paper with personal information on all of them. She walked into Sondra's office and split the stack into three piles. Sondra looked at Jan and said, "Here, take this red highlighter and mark everything you see that you think may slant someone away from Ray. Take this green highlighter and mark anything you see that might make a person favorable to Ray's case. The computer has given us its profile of these people. What I want is a review by a smart human. Find something! Find something important! This is when we earn our money."

Sondra walked to the front door and locked it from the inside. She then turned off her cell phone and suggested that everyone else do the same. They went into the conference room to study the data.

"Unless your question is very important, just make a note of it and keep the talking to a minimum until we are done," she said to Jan. "First we study this stuff, and when we are finished with the analysis, then we will talk about it. OK?"

Jan nodded. The silence of the room was broken only by the distant drone of the air conditioner, the shuffle of the papers, and the sound of a pencil, pen, or highlighter scratching an occasional note.

They broke for lunch at one o'clock and they decided to go out to clear their heads from the tedious work they had been doing. Most of the lunch crowd was leaving the restaurant as they walked in. They sat at a booth near the back when Anne spoke.

"So what do you think, Jan?"

"I think I have been rubbing a lot more red ink on those papers than green."

"Yeah, me too," chimed Sondra.

Anne nodded and optimistically said, "It's all true, but we have done some green as well."

"I can't wait until we start on the analysis," said Jan.

"Well, let's eat now and when we get back we can start on that."

"I think I'll have this club sandwich and a draught beer. Sometimes it works wonders to calm the stress level," said Sondra. Jan and Anne chose to settle for bacon, lettuce, and tomato sandwiches with iced tea to drink. After a relaxing meal, they returned to the office.

"Look through your stack of people and pick out those individuals that you think are followers and lay them aside," Sondra said. "We will be left with people who probably have strong opinions one way or the other. I think we should key on people who subscribe to political publications such as The Guardian, The Blaze, The Nation, American Rifleman, Sports Afield, The Washington Times, Rolling Stone, The Economist … you know, political stuff. What people spend money to read tells a lot about them. They must at least be interested in that point of view; otherwise, why would they pay good money to read and learn more about it?"

"I spotted one guy the other side will try to get for sure," said Jan.

"Tell me about him," spoke Anne softly.

"Number 63. He is a recent New York transplant; it says that he was a big shot with the Democratic Party in New York City. He ran for alderman twice and actually won a two-year term. He had no military service and has been divorced twice, and he subscribes to The Nation magazine. I'll have to do more research to find out how he voted and what he did. Odds are he's anti-gun, anti-conservative, and will want to nail Ray's hide to the barn door."

"That was some good work," echoed Sondra. "Put him at the top of the list to look into further."

Anne looked at Sondra and said, "Any hits?"

"Yes, I have a few here that look interesting. Number 270 is a black male, self-employed, owns a barbecue sandwich shop, he lives in a nice part of town. It is a racially mixed neighborhood, but most of the residents are white. He's a

Viet Nam veteran who enlisted into the Marines and was honorably discharged. He is registered as a Libertarian and has a subscription to the National Rifleman magazine, which means he is in the NRA. He is married and has a grown son."

"Definitely, definitely put him on the list," said Anne.

The women compared notes and selected about 50 people that they would need to study further. When they decided to break for home, night had already fallen.

The next day, five minutes before 10 a.m., Jack rolled up to the office of Hill and Dale consulting in his silver Corvette. He locked his car and walked to the front entry. As he opened the door, the sound of light conversation and the smell of fresh brewed coffee filled the air.

"Just exactly what I need, fresh coffee and a room full of pretty ladies," he said.

"We have your coffee cup right here, come and sit down," said Sondra. He picked up the black cup with the white Stetson hat on the side, the one that said GUNSLINGER, and he filled it with java.

He took a sip and generally spoke to the table, "So what have we got?"

"I have seen better," answered Anne. "We have about fifty names that we have set aside that we consider remarkable in one way or another. We don't have a lot of friendlies to choose from, but there are a few."

"It is very important that we get at least one sympathetic juror on the panel. They usually call about 25 prospects for each trial that may be called that week. Since this is such a high-profile case, Judge May will probably ask for a larger jury pool, maybe 50 to choose from. That means we might get a chance to seat two or three in the actual jury. We'll get down to a lot more detail after the clerk determines the final cut."

"Why don't we move into the conference room and you can see for yourself?" Anne asked.

"Good idea, let's go."

Jack followed the women into the conference room. As Jack studied the selected profiles, Anne quietly spoke of a new set of statistics. "Jack, there is a larger than normal list of people getting government checks in this pool, 56% overall. This would include people employed by the government, social security recipients, and, of course, other social programs such as welfare and disability." Jack listened and thought for a few seconds and then he returned to his analysis.

Without looking up, Jack asked, "What do you think about the jury size, Sondra?"

"Six," she replied. "Judge May doesn't waste time. He'll do the minimum."

"What about you, Anne?"

"I agree for a different reason. I believe that he wants a conviction. I think it will be easier with a small jury."

Jack could see the concern on Jan's face and looked right at her and said, "Keep the faith, young lady, we will get him out of jail. Just wait and see. When you talk to him, please stay optimistic. Believe me, we will prevail."

Jack continued to study the files in front of him. After an hour, he sighed and said to the women, "It looks like you have done your usual great job. I expect that the state is doing essentially the same thing, but my guess is they don't go the extra mile. The human analysis is what gives us the edge. It would be nice if this prosecutor is lazy, but with as much press as this case has generated, I expect them to field the best people that they have in the office. It may be a duel right from the start. Please keep working on the large group, but I believe we'll hit it really hard when the individual jury pools are assigned. I like the looks of numbers 18, 151, 170, 203, 270, 276 and 301. Let's have as much as you can get on these people, and keep your fingers crossed that we get at least one into the jury."

CHAPTER 15

SELECTING THE JURY

The bailiff walked out to the bar in the courtroom filled with potential jurors and instructed them to answer the questions posed by the attorneys truthfully when asked. He then walked over and opened the door to the judge's chambers and waved his hand toward the judge. The judge, who was on the telephone, acknowledged his presence by holding up five fingers, meaning he would be there in five minutes. The bailiff understood, nodded, and closed the door. Then he walked to the center of the courtroom and asked if anyone had any questions or wanted to request an exemption for cause; several people raised their hands and requested to speak with the clerk of court. The clerk's secretary led the line of people out of the courtroom. The bailiff then said that the judge would give the jury pool specific instructions shortly.

The door to the judge's chambers opened and Judge May entered the courtroom.

The bailiff barked, "All rise!" and the jurors did as they were told.

Judge May said, "You will be asked to take a seat in the jury box as you are called. The lawyers and I will ask you questions. You are required to answer them honestly and you are required to follow my instructions. Do you understand? Are there any questions?"

There were no hands raised. As the bailiff called off the first twelve names, the seats in the jury box began to fill. Frances James and her assistants filled the table to the right and Jack Edwards and Anne Hill took notes behind the other. As they sifted through the first twenty-five jurors, the defense managed to seat two people selected from their list of green highlighted friendlies. However, the prosecution also seated two jurors who had been in Anne's stack of remarkable people. The jurors chosen by Frances James were people who had been highlighted in red. The last two regular jurors came from the large group of people who were considered by Hill and Dale to be average, independent, and unremarkable.

Now the six primary and two alternate jurors had been chosen. It was time for the trial to begin.

CHAPTER 16

THE TRIAL

Many people stood outside of the elevator trying to make their way to the courtroom located on the eighth floor. They hoped to secure a seat in the courtroom to witness the trial. Most of the available seats were taken by the major news media, the staff and assistants for the counsel, and the friends and families of the men who were killed or injured by Ray Jordan. The bailiff had been ordered by the court to see to it that the people directly involved with the case and the media would have the best seats available in each day's proceedings. The remaining seats were given out in a first-come, first-served basis in the gallery. A closed-circuit television system had been installed and the proceedings were being viewed as they happened in a meeting room located on the first floor near the building entrance.

Ivory Franklin was accompanied by his mother and a burly young man pushing his wheelchair. As they entered the courtroom, several members of the news media took notice of the well-groomed young man accompanied by his mother and what looked like a male nurse or attendant. The court artist made a sketch of the trio as they found their places in the first row behind the prosecution team. The orchid hat and dress of Bernese Franklin and the urine bag hanging under Ivory's wheelchair were prominently featured in the artist's rendering.

The bailiff stepped out of the short hallway and spoke into the din of the packed courtroom, "Hear ye … Hear ye … Hear ye, the Honorable Peter J. May!"

Judge May, taking long strides, stormed across the courtroom with his usual amount of flair. As he sat down, the buzz that had so recently filled the air turned to silence punctuated by the sound of a few still cameras capturing the trial for the history books. The jury members filed in and took their assigned seats.

At one minute past nine a.m., Judge May peered over his glasses and asked Frances James, "Is the prosecution ready to proceed?"

"Yes, Your Honor."

Glancing to the right, the judge locked eyes with Jack Edwards and said simply, "Mr. Edwards?"

"Yes, Your Honor, the defense is ready."

"Ms. James, do you have an opening statement?"

"Yes, Your Honor. Thank you."

Frances James walked to the center near the jury box. She wore a classy muted red business suit with matching high heels that accentuated her well-toned body. She smiled and studied the jury's faces before she said, "The prosecution intends to show that Mr. Ray Jordan wantonly and unnecessarily took the lives of two innocent young men and seriously injured a third youth." She paused briefly to let her words sink in. "We intend to show that these acts were racially motivated and that the actions of Mr. Ray Jordan were precipitated by a harmless prank, which he clearly used as an excuse to execute these unarmed young black men. The State of Florida is aware that Mr. Jordan lost his wife as a result of this incident, and we wish to extend our condolences to him at this time. However, having said that, we ask you, the members of the jury, to remember that the accidental death of his wife does not excuse his actions on that fateful day. This is not the Old West, where vengeance is played out with guns on our city streets. We are a lawful society. We have remedies for 'accidents' in civil court. We are a civilized people. We don't kill others because they have made a mistake or used poor judgment. Thank You, Your Honor." Frances James turned from the jury and returned to her table.

"Mr. Edwards?" Judge May said.

"Thank you Your Honor, I'll be brief. Ours is a simple task. First, I wish to thank the prosecution for making this trial about race. We were aware from the very beginning that this was a case where race would play a major role. Had this shooting been black on black or white on white, I suspect there would be empty seats in this courtroom, but here we are with the news media from all around the world reporting." He gestured around the room with his hand and paused for a moment. "A prank turned bad by innocent teens. It's hard not to feel sympathy for the victims in this case. Isn't it? Well, it is my job is to put you there, in Ray Jordan's shoes, and to show you that the scene that the prosecution and the media have been, and will be, painting is all fiction. A lie. I will demonstrate how, right up until the utterance of what were clearly racially-charged 'fighting words,' Ray Jordan was coping with the loss of his wife in a caring, loving manner. It was not until the occupants of the green Hummer hurled insults and celebrated the murder of his wife that he resorted to violence. A justifiable form of violence. A rational form of violence, and a defensive form of violence. Yes, he struck out, just like most people would, and he fought back when he was assaulted. That is normal. A totally sane, normal, and predictable reaction to 'fighting words' after the senseless killing of his wife of forty years." Jack lowered his voice and continued. "He is not a man who belongs in the penitentiary." Jack nodded at the jury and moved to his seat.

The judge looked down on the courtroom and said, "Will the prosecution please call their first witness?"

"The Prosecution calls Sergeant George La Monica to the stand."

As the witness took the stand, the bailiff administered his oath and the judge asked him to identify himself for the court reporter. Shortly thereafter, Frances James walked to the center of the courtroom and asked, "Sergeant, were you the first policeman to arrive at the scene of the shooting?"

"Yes, my partner and I were the first to arrive."

"Approximately how long did it take you to arrive at the murder scene on Twelfth Street?"

George thought for a moment and said, "From the time that we received the call to the time we arrived at the intersection, it was roughly six or seven minutes."

"Can you describe what you saw? What were your first impressions when you first rolled up?"

"Sure. I saw several people huddled together in the crosswalk, probably eight or ten in all. They seemed to be mostly women, and they began to disburse in every direction almost immediately after they saw us."

"Did you get enough of a look at these women to describe what they looked like?"

"Yes I did. They all were dark-skinned and some looked as though they were wearing a type of uniform, perhaps that of a hotel worker."

"Were you able to see Mr. Jordan?"

"Not immediately, but after the women who were helping him moved away, he was clearly visible."

"Please continue."

"There were two people remaining in the crosswalk when we exited our patrol unit; one was kneeling and one was prone. The kneeling man was holding a woman's upper body. I also noticed a green Hummer that had crept forward into the intersection and was stopped against the curb. I also saw a wounded man lying in the cross street who was calling out for help."

"What were your actions at that time?"

"I knew that there had been a shooting and I first wanted to secure the weapons that remained at the scene."

"Can you describe how that was done?"

"Yes, I can. I pointed my service pistol at the man who was kneeling in the street and asked him if he was armed."

"And what happened next?"

"He raised his left hand and lifted the bottom of his shirt with his right hand to reveal a pistol concealed in his waistband."

"Did he indicate that he wanted you to take it?"

"Yes, he made a nodding gesture and stood stone still."

"Was he aggressive?"

"No ma'am, he looked and acted very subdued. I had him face away from me and remain on his knees and I then took possession of his weapon. My partner handcuffed him and took him into custody."

"Do you recognize the man you took into custody inside this courtroom?"

"Yes I do, he is seated at the table right there."

"Let the record show that the witness has indicated the gunman as being Ray Jordan, the defendant in this case. Sergeant, does this look like the gun you took from Mr. Jordan?"

"Yes, that looks like the weapon."

"Are you sure, sergeant?"

"Yes, that is the one that I took from him. These particular guns are more than one hundred years old and quite sought after by collectors. The sleek design of them is unmistakable."

"Thank you, sergeant." She held the clear plastic bag containing the gun in her right hand and said, "Your Honor, I place this Colt 1903 pistol into evidence."

Turning her attention back to the witness, she said, "What did you do after Ray Jordan was arrested?"

"I quickly moved to the wounded man on the side street and tried to locate his weapon and attend to his wounds."

"Very well, sergeant. Were you able to find the man's weapon?"

"No ma'am."

"Sergeant, are you testifying that the wounded man you found bleeding from a pair of gunshot wounds was unarmed?"

"Yes I am."

"So sergeant, after you found that the wounded man was unarmed," she paused for effect, "how did you attend to his wounds?"

Before he could answer the question, Frances James raised her hand to the witness asking him to stop speaking, and she turned and looked directly at the jury in an effort to accentuate his previous answer. Returning her gaze to the witness, he continued, "Well, I tried to administer first aid, but mostly I tried to keep him aware of his surroundings and assure him that help was on the way. It is very important to try to minimize the shock to a gunshot victim."

"How long were you with the wounded man?"

"Probably less than one minute. The Emergency Medical Team arrived shortly after I got to him and they took over his care."

"Did that conclude your investigation?"

"No ma'am."

"Can you please describe what you did next?"

"Yes ma'am. I met up with my partner outside of the green Hummer."

"Can you please describe what you saw?"

"Yes, it was obvious that there had been a homicide inside of the car. There were two black men who had been shot dead. One man was in the front driver's seat and one man was located behind him in the back driver's side seat."

"Were you able to determine how they had been killed?"

"Yes, they were both shot in the head."

"Sergeant, did you locate a weapon on or near either one of these men?"

"Not immediately, by that I mean there was no gun in view, but after forensics had finished with their job, we did locate a Taurus .40 caliber pistol inside of the console."

"Had the gun been fired?"

"The gun had a loaded hollow point round in the chamber and a full magazine. That would indicate to me that the gun had probably not been fired."

"So sergeant, is it your testimony that none of the men in the Hummer were armed or fired a gun at the defendant?"

"Well, I wasn't there, but given the evidence that we uncovered at the scene I would have to agree that nothing that I saw indicated that anyone inside the Hummer had fired at Mr. Jordan."

"Is there anything else that you remember about the Hummer?"

"Yes, I noticed that both passenger-side doors were open and that there was very little blood found inside the car."

"Thank you, sergeant. Your witness."

Jack Edwards walked close to the witness stand and asked, "Sergeant La Monica, I just want to touch on a couple of things that you testified to."

"Yes sir."

"Did you say that you recovered a Taurus pistol from the Hummer?"

"Yes sir, a .40 caliber."

"In your expert opinion, would you say that a forty caliber would be a pretty formidable weapon?"

"Yes sir, many police departments and the government use the forty for their forces."

"Did you have a chance to run the serial numbers on that particular weapon?"

"Objection, Your Honor!" Frances James leapt to her feet. "What does it matter what the serial number is on the man's gun? These men are not on trial here! Please, Your Honor, let us not forget that these young men are the victims."

"Objection sustained, Mr. Edwards. The court will not allow you to impugn the reputation of those who have been killed and wounded in this case. The witness has already testified that the gun was not fired during the incident, making the driver's gun irrelevant!"

Jack turned towards the jury box and answered, "Yes, Your Honor. We all seek justice."

Judge May looked down with a disapproving sneer and said, "You may proceed with the witness."

Turning his attention back to the stand, Jack continued, "Sergeant La Monica, how many doors were open on the passenger side of the Hummer when you first inspected the car?"

"Both doors, sir."

Jack echoed, "Both doors?"

"Yes, *both* doors."

"When you arrived at the scene and went to render aid to the downed man on the side street, did you notice on his body where his injuries were located?"

"Yes, he had a bleeding injury that we later identified as a gunshot wound near the abdomen."

"Could you tell how many times he had been hit?"

"No sir, I couldn't tell. He still had his clothes on when I saw him."

"Can you describe how the man acted?"

"Yes, at the time, he was in great distress and he had been bleeding quite a bit."

"Was the blood localized to his abdomen?"

"No, he had been clutching at his wounds and he had a good deal of blood on his arms and hands."

"Did you notice if he was tested for gunshot residue traces on his clothes and hands?"

"I did not notice at the time, but I have looked into the matter and I know now that he was not tested. I assume that because no gun was found with him, the test was never performed. I simply saw him being loaded aboard the first ambulance along with the body of Caroline Jordan and they were off to the hospital and then on to the morgue."

"Do you recognize the wounded man here in the courtroom?"

"Yes, he is seated in the wheelchair right behind the prosecutor."

"Did you testify earlier that the car, the Hummer, had very little blood inside?"

"Yes, I did."

"In your informed opinion, how do you suppose two men can be shot to death and a third severely injured inside of a car and there be very little blood found in the immediate area?"

"Well, in my opinion, I would say that the two people who were found inside the car were killed instantly and the third, the wounded man, was outside of the car when his injuries were sustained."

"Thank you, sergeant."

Jack Edwards walked to the jury box and turned to face the witness. "Sergeant, had you ever seen Ray Jordan before?"

"No, sir. He was a total stranger."

"Had you ever seen Rondell Macdume, Demontre Powell, or Ivory Franklin before?"

"Objection, objection, Your Honor!" Frances James sighed and looked pleadingly at the judge as he admonished the defense.

"How many times do I have to tell you that these men are not on trial in this courtroom? The objection is sustained again. Mr. Edwards, your reputation precedes you. I know that you know better than to act like this. I want to point out that this is only our first witness and you have already broken with protocol on two occasions. You had better stop this line of questioning or you will find yourself in contempt of my court, I don't care who you are!"

Like water off a duck's back, Jack looked up and agreed with the judge, "Yes, Your Honor. May I continue?"

The judge did not speak but waved his hand, gesturing towards the witness.

"Turning our attention to Mr. Jordan, sergeant, you have testified that he was cooperative and subdued, is that correct?"

"Yes. Yes he was."

"Can you think of any other words that you might use to describe his demeanor?"

"Yes he looked befuddled and confused, and I would say that he was very sad."

"Would you also say that he was holding back information or tried to mislead you in any way?"

"No, no sir, he was very forthcoming with his answers, and I am sure that he was aware of his Miranda rights because I read them to him myself."

"Sergeant, did he incriminate himself in the shooting?"

"Yes he did."

Jack looked at the jury and repeated, "He did not deny that he was the man who pulled the trigger. Now then, sergeant, did he mention a fourth passenger who ran off with a chrome revolver?"

"Yes he did. He was quite adamant about it."

"Did he say that he was fired upon by one of the Hummer's occupants with that chrome revolver?"

"Yes he did, right from the start."

Looking again at the jury, Jack repeated while pointing at Ray, "This man has admitted the shooting and has held from the very beginning that he was being fired upon by Ivory Franklin over the top of the Hummer."

He turned from the jury box and said, "Thank you, sergeant. Your Honor, I have no more questions for this witness at this time." Judge May peered down from above and said, "Thank you, sergeant, you may step down."

In an unusual strategy, Jack made Ray available for testimony. The prosecution called Ray Jordan to the stand.

Ray looked at Jack and walked to the fore of the court, placed his hand on the Bible and swore to tell the truth. The judge directed Ray to be seated in the witness stand. Judge May then looked down and said, "Mr. Jordan, have you discussed the issue of giving testimony in your own trial with your counsel?"

"I have, Your Honor."

"And are you fully aware that it is not necessary for you to take the stand?"

"Yes sir, I am aware."

"You understand that the prosecution must prove beyond a reasonable doubt that you are guilty of this crime and, if they fail to do so, you will not be convicted."

"Yes, judge, I am aware."

In a moment of rare compassion, the judge said again, "I feel that it is my duty to make absolutely certain that you understand that anything you may say can and will be used against you."

"Thank you, sir. I know that it is a risk for me to take the stand, but there are things that I would like to say to the jury and sitting quietly at the table will not allow me to do so."

Judge May looked down and said, "Very well then, if you have something you want to say, let us proceed. Ms. James, please begin."

"Mr. Jordan, why were you carrying that gun under your shirt?"

Ray thought for a moment and answered, "I always carry a gun. I consider it a kind of insurance policy."

"An insurance policy. What kind of insurance policy would that be, Mr. Jordan?"

"The gun that I carry insures me against being assaulted or robbed by people much stronger and more physically fit than myself."

"So, Mr. Jordan, how did Rondell, Demontre, and Ivory assault you? It looks to me like they never even got out of their car."

"Rondell did more than assault us; he actually killed my wife. He assaulted us by driving very close to us with his big car and blasting his train whistle horn at my wife and me so loudly that it caused us physical pain. It was an assault serious enough to scare my wife to death. The noise from that train horn was so startling that my poor wife's heart quit beating. It was a mean and deliberate assault. I saw it that way then and I see it that way now. Demontre assaulted us by the words that he spoke, words that were insulting and defaming to my dying wife. He verbally poked a stick in my eye as I was tending to the final moments of my wife's life. Ivory was actively trying to kill us. He fired at me three times with a very powerful chrome revolver. I feared for my life and considered it a clear-cut assault with an unmistakable intent to kill us. In his case, I was simply defending myself against him."

Looking mockingly at the jury, Frances snidely repeated, "Oh yes, the chrome revolver. Perhaps I missed it, Mr. Jordan, but I didn't see a chrome revolver placed into evidence. Where is it, sir?"

"The fourth man took it and ran into the crowd near the corner."

She then smiled at the jury and said in a derisive manner, "That is very *convenient* for you. A mystery gun, taken by a mystery man. Although there were dozens of witnesses, nobody interviewed heard the shots, or saw the gun or the mystery man running into the crowd. In his deposition, Ivory Franklin has testified that there were only three people inside of the Hummer. Do you really expect the jury to value your story more than his?"

Ray answered back, "You asked me for the truth and I gave it to you."

Jack stood up and said, "Objection, Your Honor, the prosecution is badgering the witness!"

Without hesitation, Judge May slapped down the gavel and said, "Overruled."

Frances James continued by asking, "Mr. Jordan, how is it that most people who live in America go through their lives and never need your kind of insurance policy?"

"You are asking me to speculate?"

"Yes I am, sir."

"Well, people insure for things they never use all the time. In fact most people hope they never use their insurance. Think about it. Almost everyone has fire insurance on their house, but how often is it ever used?"

"I'm speaking of guns now, sir, not fire insurance! Please explain to the jury why *you* in particular need to carry a gun when most people do not!"

"I can't honestly answer that question, ma'am. I don't know what motivates other people to do what they do, but I have heard that nearly one person in ten carry a gun here in Florida. While that is not a majority of your residents, it seems like an awful lot of people to me."

"You have still not given me a reason for having this need, this paranoia to constantly have deadly force at your fingertips."

"Objection, Your Honor, the question is prejudicial."

Looking annoyed, Judge May repeated, "Overruled. Please answer the question."

"Speaking for myself, I just want to keep breathing. It is simply basic self-preservation. I am a firm believer of the old adage that it is better to have a gun and not need it than to need it and not have it. I have always trusted myself to use this force with prudence."

Thinking that Ray had stepped into a trap, Frances James asked, "So in order for you to 'keep breathing,' you found it necessary to stop two young men from breathing, isn't that so?"

"Yes ma'am. I didn't want to do it but those are the undeniable facts," spoke Ray. "Sometimes it is necessary to have to do that very thing. I heard them laughing and mocking my dying wife. I just sort of reacted to the circumstances."

"Mr. Jordan, can you explain how you felt when you gunned down these men?"

"Objection, Your Honor."

"Overruled. Mr. Jordan, please answer the question."

"I really can't."

"What do you mean, you can't!"

"In retrospect, I can't pin down a particular feeling that I had. It seemed to me that I momentarily flashed back to my last day of combat in Viet Nam. It was when I was wounded and lost consciousness. I had sort of lost control over my body and the events that took place were more or less automatic."

"So you went crazy?"

"No, I wouldn't call it crazy. I just felt kind of numb and sort of helpless. I don't really know how to describe it to your satisfaction, but I am trying the best that I can. Strangely enough, after my hand touched the gun, I became calm and detached from the world that surrounded me."

"So Mr. Jordan, would it be correct to say that while you shot these men, you were calm and detached?"

"Yes, I suppose it would be so. My existence at that time was in my hands. I had control of my future."

"Please try to explain to me how you can say that you were helpless when you had the power in your hand to, in fact, kill two men? Are you sure that helpless is the correct feeling?"

"I was helpless in the sense that my conscious mind had sort of shut down and I was reacting in a purely uninhibited way. It was like I was suddenly uncivilized and my mind had reverted to a kill or be killed frame. The only other time I have had that feeling was when I was under attack in Viet Nam."

"Mr. Jordan, if you had to do it over, would you have acted in the same way, or would you have called the police and let them administer justice to the men in the Hummer?"

"You mean, if they had killed my wife?"

"Yes, Mr. Jordan, if your wife had passed."

"I am positive that I would have acted in the same way."

"Ladies and gentlemen of the jury, he just said that he would do it again! Mr. Jordan, it seems as though you live in an alternate universe, perhaps one hundred years in the past, where there is one marshal to serve hundreds of miles of wilderness and a man must kill to live. This is here in Miami, Florida, right now, with a policeman at nearly every street corner and a surveillance video at almost every traffic light. It is obvious that you are not sorry for what you have done, am I correct?"

"Yes ma'am, you are correct."

"Would you consider your actions prudent?"

"Yes I would."

Muttering to herself, she said, "You are too much, Mr. Jordan." Looking up, Frances James said, "Your Honor, this man has admitted guilt and has shown absolutely no remorse. Not only that, he has indicated that if the circumstances were duplicated that he would take even more life. I move that we release the jury from its duties and move right into the penalty stage of this trial."

Jack stood up and the judge motioned for him to relax. "Ms. James, are you the new judge here?" Frances sheepishly looked at the judge as he said, "You will see this trial all the way through, counselor, and we, along with this jury, will bring it to a just conclusion. There will be nothing of this sort done in my courtroom."

Sensing she had inflicted severe damage to Ray, she looked at Jack Edwards and said, "Your witness."

Addressing the jury, Jack said, "Let's talk about people who carry guns. I'll bet you without even knowing that every person sitting at the prosecution table belongs to the same alternate universe that Ray Jordan belongs to. I know for a fact that everyone at my table belongs to it! My guess is that at least one of you belongs to it as well. If you are, Ms. James just maligned you. Is that how you think? Are you looking for trouble every time you leave the house, or are you simply responsibly prepared for a bad event that may take place in your presence? To infer that there is no crime in Miami because there is a policeman at every street corner and surveillance video at every traffic light is the height of folly. We have heard testimony that the first police to arrive at the scene took seven minutes. I am an old man and I can run a mile in seven minutes. Is the prosecution retaining an exculpatory video? If there is a camera at every street corner like she said, then where is the video? I want to see it! We can end this trial right now. Come on, allow us see it! Miami, it seems, has a pretty consistent record of making the top ten crime cities in the nation as often as not. Do you think the safe city idea might be a bit of an exaggeration?"

Moving over to the stand, Jack began to question Ray.

"Mr. Jordan, when you were at home in Wyoming, how often did you go out without a weapon?"

"Never. It is like a belt. If I am not in the shower, I have it on."

"Did you have a concealed weapons license in California when you were younger?"

"Yes I did."

"Was it easy to get?"

"No sir, it took a letter from the Governor, a good reason, and a complete FBI background check to get it."

"So why did they give you one?"

"We did a lot of work in some pretty sketchy places near the docks. I always felt that trustworthy people in my organization should have the ability to protect the crew if we had jobs to do at night or in particularly high-crime areas. I included myself in the group of trustworthy employees and apparently the governor and the FBI agreed."

"So about how many years have you been carrying a weapon?"

"You mean, as a civilian?"

"Yes, outside of the military."

"Probably near forty years."

"More than half your life?"

"Yes sir."

"How many times have you pulled your gun in anger?"

"Never."

"Have you ever used your gun at all in a personal defense way?"

"Twice in California."

"Please explain to the jury the circumstances that prompted you to actually use your weapon."

"I used it once to deter a robbery at an automated teller machine late one night and one other time to hold a suspect in an attempted rape until the police arrived."

"Did you shoot those people?"

"No sir. I didn't need to."

"The prosecution has painted you as a remorseless killer. Do you feel that way?"

"As I have said to her, it is difficult for me to answer many of her questions."

"Please explain yourself."

"Simply said, I am a lover of life and go out of my way to help people and animals when they are in need. I certainly didn't want for this to happen. I am a firm believer that people should be free to do as they want so long as it doesn't hurt other people. But in this case, people were hurt and those people were my wife and me. I admit to being remorseless because I did the right thing. I believed it then and I believe it now. Do I think it is my place to right all the wrongs in the world? No I don't. Do I think that it is my business to correct and punish people like Rondell? Not really. It wasn't until they made it my business that I was compelled to respond. They got what was coming to them. I do not feel remorse for this action, but I don't really feel anger, either. I think simply that justice was served. As for being a killer, that's a hard one. Technically I guess I am, but I am not a murderer. I know the difference and I am not a murderer."

"Tell me, Ray, if your wife had not been fatally injured by the horn blast, would you have gotten angry?"

"I suspect that I would have. Yes, probably so."

"Would you have pulled your weapon?"

"No, I know better than to reach for a gun when I am angry. I may have cussed him out, but if she had been OK, I am certain we would have continued on our way to the theatre. It would have made no sense for me to take on four young men who were obviously bigger and stronger than me."

"Ray, earlier in your testimony you touched upon your service in Viet Nam. You said that your mind flashed back to your last battle, is that correct?"

"Yes sir, it was a scene I'll never forget."

"Can you describe it for the court?"

"We were on patrol near the DMZ and started taking on fire. There was this guy named Art Ellis that used to travel pretty close to me. He was hit and wounded right away. I took cover behind some trees nearby. I noticed that he was continuing to receive enemy fire and he was calling for me to help him. I left my rifle behind and ran to carry him to cover. I was hit on my way back. I don't remember much more after that until Art and I were on the medevac chopper and on our way back to the base."

"Is that the scene you saw in your mind when the shooting occurred?"

"Yes it was."

"You appear to be a very well-adjusted man, Ray. Did you have any PTSD issues after you became a civilian?"

"I did, but I handled them myself."

"What do you mean when you say that you handled it yourself?"

"That means my wife and I talked about it and, after a while, with her guidance, I was able to put it behind me."

"I suspect that the event that you just described would be your most traumatic event. Is that so?"

"No sir. Not even close. I was hit and somewhat unconscious. Others cared for me and then I was safe. No, not even close to LZ Fox."

"Can you tell us about your experience there?"

Ray took a moment to compose himself and then he began, "We were tasked with securing and guarding a very important landing zone. When I knew that I was going to be in one place for a while I always dug a hole in the ground near some cover. I shaped it sort of like a recliner chair and when night would fall I would lie down in the hole and place my rifle across my chest. I would cover myself with tree limbs or vegetation and wait for the sun to come up. I don't know how they did it, but somehow the VC slipped through the perimeter and killed almost everybody in the battalion. I used up nearly all of my ammunition during the battle, but they were well prepared and there were a lot of them. When reinforcements started to arrive, they disappeared into the jungle where they came from. I stayed in the hole until the sun came up and I could hear some of the other survivors speaking English."

There was silence in the courtroom for a few moments and then Jack asked, "What did you think of yourself after that incident?"

"I considered myself to be a stealthy killing machine. Yes, they were able to slip into our camp, but after that I learned that I could be more effective than even I could believe, and after surviving LZ Fox, I believed I was invincible."

Jack scanned the jury and noticed that Mose was visibly touched by Ray's testimony. After feeling that he had successfully anchored the necessary juror to win the case, he concluded his questions for Ray.

"I thank you for your candor and truthfulness. We sometimes have to pry honesty from our witnesses but you have frankly and willingly answered everything we have asked. I am finished, Your Honor."

"The witness may step down."

After a one-hour recess, the testimony continued. The prosecution called Dr. David Lee to the stand.

Dr. Lee walked to the witness stand. He was dressed in a pair of khaki pants and a light blue shirt with a dark blue tie. His shoes were shined and his demeanor was very professional.

Frances James walked to the witness and asked, "Dr. Lee, are you the medical examiner for Dade County, Florida?"

"I am the chief pathologist for Dade County. We have more than one medical examiner. I am the head of the Medical Examiner's office."

"Earlier this year, did you examine the bodies of Rondell Macdume and Demontre Powell?"

"Yes, I did."

"In the course of the autopsy, were you able to determine the cause of death?"

"Yes ma'am."

"Please tell the court what you found."

"The primary cause of death to Rondell Macdume was damage to the frontal lobe of the brain."

"Were you able to determine what caused this damage to the brain?"

"Yes, it was a single .32 caliber bullet."

She continued, "Was there more than one injury to the brain?"

"Well, yes and no, not life-threatening damage but some head trauma."

"What do you mean, doctor?"

"Rondell had signs of skull fractures that had happened sometime in the past, perhaps even as far back as childhood, that had healed."

"Is that a danger?"

"Brain injuries are always dangerous. They sometimes weaken the vessels in the damaged areas and rupture at later times. They can also sometimes spark personality changes due to the damage."

"Did it look like this had happened?"

"No, it didn't, but you asked and I simply wanted to completely answer your question to the best of my ability."

"So you are saying that his skull was not perfect before the gunshot?"

"Yes, in fact it looked like someone or some thing had done some serious damage to his head when he was younger."

"Dr. Lee, would you conclude, in the end, that the .32 caliber gunshot to the head was the cause of death for Rondell Macdume?"

"Yes ma'am, no question."

"Dr. Lee, did you also report on the death of Demontre Powell?"

"Yes I did."

"What were your findings regarding his cause of death?"

"Demontre had two injuries to the head. There were small fragments of glass in the wounds. The first injury was a laceration near the back of the skull caused by a bullet that had hit and not penetrated the cranium. The second injury entered the soft tissue in front of the ear and damaged the temporal area of the brain, causing almost instant death."

"Dr. Lee, did you recover the bullets from Demontre Powell?"

"Yes, I did."

"Did they match the bullet taken from Rondell Macdume?"

"Yes, the ballistics lab said that they were fired from the same gun. The one bullet that did not penetrate was located but badly misshapen. However, the lands and grooves did indicate that it was fired from the same gun."

"Thank you, Dr. Lee. Your witness."

Jack Edwards greeted Dr. Lee with a confident smile and said, "Good morning, Dr. Lee. Tell us, doctor, how long have you been examining corpses and determining the cause of death for the county?"

"I started back in the mid 1980s so I would say it would have to be nearly 30 years."

Jack looked at the jury and repeated, "Thirty years. I suspect that in that time you have seen quite a few homicides committed with firearms."

"Yes I have, many."

"By many do you mean a dozen? A hundred? A thousand?"

"I'm sure the number would be more than a thousand."

"Using your vast experience, doctor, would you conclude that the wounds created by this .32 caliber gun were severe?"

Dr. Lee seemed puzzled by the question and repeated, "Severe?"

Jack cleared his throat and said, "Let me be more specific. What I mean is, how do these .32 caliber wounds compare with, say, a .40 caliber or a .45 or just your average everyday gun homicide?"

Dr. Lee seemed relieved and spoke, "These wounds were unusually small in size. I would have to say that they were far less severe than the bullet injuries that we see almost every day."

"Please say that again, doctor."

"The wounds were far less severe than the ones I usually see in the morgue."

Jack looked at the jury and repeated, "Far less severe than the average wound he sees." Jack turned his attention to Dr. Lee and said, "What was different about these wounds that would make them 'less severe' than your normal gun homicide?"

"These bullets were fired from a small caliber rather weak pistol, and the bullets that were recovered were full metal jacket basic target ammunition. The normal gun homicide is generally done with a much larger gun using ammunition specifically made to exact maximum tissue damage."

"So then, Dr. Lee, if this gun is so weak and ineffective, why are these two men dead?"

"Shot placement, in my best estimation. The only thing I can conclude is that Mr. Jordan was either very lucky or he is an excellent marksman. He was able to place his shots in the most vital and unprotected areas of the deceased. I speculate that if these bullets had hit almost anywhere else, they would have only produced superficial wounds such as those incurred by Ivory Franklin."

"Earlier today we heard the testimony of Sergeant George La Monica. He testified that there was very little blood found inside the vehicle where these men were shot dead. He concluded that because the shots had hit vital areas, that the deaths were nearly instantaneous. Do you agree with that conclusion?"

"Yes I do."

"Is there any other explanation for the lack of blood that you can think of?"

"No, not really. When the heart stops, the blood flow stops shortly after. It's simple biology."

"So doctor, would you conclude, relying on your thirty plus years of experience, that the gun that Ray Jordan used was basically an antique and purely a defensive weapon?"

"Yes, I would have to agree. I know, and see firsthand, that there are many other bullet types and calibers that are commonly available that would have been far more destructive."

"So, doctor, does it make sense for a man who is quote 'looking for trouble' or targeting someone to kill, to choose to use such a weak and ineffective gun?"

"Objection, Your Honor. He is a forensic doctor, not a mind reader!"

"Sustained."

"Dr. Lee, are these reports #56218 and 56219 your complete conclusion about the autopsies of the two men?"

"Yes they are."

"I direct your attention to paragraph four titled 'toxicology' of both reports."

"Objection, Your Honor!" This time Frances James was red in the face. Her fury was obvious. "The defense is trying to prejudice the jury!"

Judge May raises a hand as if to tell both parties to quiet down and picked up a copy of the report. He studied it for a long minute, then looked at Jack Edwards and said that her objection was sustained.

Showing no passion, Jack looked up and said, "Your Honor, the report speaks to the obvious frame of mind of the occupants inside of the Hummer."

Judge May looked down with an annoyed expression and said, "I will grant you that it might speak to the frame of mind of the occupants. I don't believe that it is obvious and I don't believe that it is pertinent to this trial. Please continue."

"Dr. Lee, earlier in your testimony you said that most of the gun homicides that you deal with are done with more powerful weapons and with more lethal ammunition. Is that so?"

"Yes, almost exclusively."

"So would you then conclude that the gun found in the Hummer, the .40 caliber with hollow point ammunition, would have been a far more lethal round?"

"Objection, Your Honor!"

"Question withdrawn. Dr. Lee, I have no more questions at this time."

"Redirect," shouted Ms. James, "Your Honor?"

"OK but keep it short," Judge May said.

"Thank you. Dr. Lee, do you know where the Taurus pistol was found?"

"No ma'am, I do not."

"Do you know if it had been fired?"

"No, I do not. I do know that no one that I examined had been shot with a .40 caliber."

Frances James then said, "Thank you, Dr. Lee," while looking directly at the jury.

And so it went. The prosecution brought testimony from the other policemen at the scene. They brought forward paid experts to fortify their point of view. Of course, the defense did the same; there were behavioral psychologists, PTSD experts, grief counselors and others to persuade the jury to see their side of the argument. The judge continued to sustain the objections of the state and to overrule the objections of the defense. As the testimony was beginning to conclude, the defense called Jay Elliano.

After swearing in, Jack Edwards asked the witness to, "Please state your name and your business."

"My name is Jay Elliano and I own Hillcrest Private Detective Agency."

"Were you hired by the firm of Edwards and Bloodworth to do some undercover work for us related to this trial?"

"Yes, I was."

"In the course of your investigation, did you uncover any information that might, in some way, impact the outcome of this trial?"

"I'm not sure if it would impact the outcome, but it is pertinent, and I believe, important information."

Jack Edwards stopped his line of questioning to look up at the judge and said, "Your Honor, Mr. Elliano has gone undercover and has produced a video that shows deceit relative to the prosecution of this trial."

The judge, with a puzzled look, queried the State, "Ms. James, are you aware of any dirty tricks or deceit from the prosecution?"

"No, Your Honor."

"Then proceed, Mr. Edwards. I won't have any hint of impropriety being done inside of my courtroom. I won't stand for it!"

"Thank you, Your Honor."

Jack turned his attention to the stand and asked, "Mr. Elliano, can you tell me about your surveillance?"

Jay nodded and spoke clearly towards the jury. "In anticipation of this trial, I have been watching Ivory Franklin for roughly the past thirty days."

"And what did you find?"

"I determined that Ivory Franklin is not disabled."

Jack pointed to the man in the wheelchair and asked, "That Ivory Franklin?"

"Yes sir, he is the one I have been watching."

Ivory looked at his mother, then he looked down at the floor.

"Mr. Elliano, what were the findings of your investigation?"

"I found that Ivory, while outside at home, almost always sat in his wheelchair. When Ivory's mother would take him away to other locations, Ivory walked without aid."

"Is that all that he did?"

"No sir, I have video of him dancing rather vigorously at the Club Ember on Walnut Street and playing basketball at the park near Seventeenth Avenue on most Wednesday nights."

Jack looked to the judge and said, "Your honor, I would like to place into evidence the video that Mr. Elliano has prepared for us."

"Not so fast, counselor. Nothing is going into evidence until I see it and approve. It is ten thirty. The court will stand in recess until one o'clock this afternoon so that counsel from both sides and I can review the new evidence." Judge May slapped down the gavel and said to the jury, "Please have a good lunch and I instruct you not to discuss this trial with anyone, including your fellow jurors, during the break. Thank you."

As Judge May left the courtroom, several of the news media begin to badger the Franklins. Bernese waved her hands back and forth like she was shooing mosquitoes to clear a path for her son and his 'nurse.'

Peter May had shed his robe and sat down behind his desk. His holstered stainless Colt Mustang government model was in plain view hanging from his belt. The judge noticed that Jack stared at his obvious hypocrisy, so he said, "Hey, I am a sworn officer of the court. I can carry if I want to." Getting back to business, he looked at Frances James and said, "What the hell is going on here? This guy is fine and you let him roll in here like he was permanently injured from that pea shooter?"

She answered, "With God as my witness, I didn't know."

The judge said, "You damn well should have known! What kind of bush league talent have you got in your office? You know this will probably impact this trial outcome and it makes the state look like a bunch of buffoons."

Her face flushed. She felt humiliated and embarrassed at the judge's frank statements and quietly agreed, "It might. It just might."

"So Mr. Elliano, let's take a look at this damn thing." Jay walked to the judge's side and opened a laptop computer. He made a few clicks with the keyboard and the video appeared. Jay Elliano was dressed as a homeless man in dirty clothes and a three-day beard, pushing a half-empty grocery cart that held a dirty quilt and a paper bag with an amber bottle inside. He had a removable tattoo on his cheek with a tear and a star below his right eye. The video panned to a fairly new two-door Buick that picked up Ivory. After furtively looking around, Ivory stood up from the wheelchair and, while the passenger opened the door and stepped out, Ivory flipped the seat forward and climbed right into the back seat. Shortly after, they drove off.

The next video showed Ivory a week later at a party at the Club Ember. The judge inquired, "How did you get this, Jay?"

"Well I didn't want to be left behind, so I took on a beard disguise and followed the car. He had been going out about three days per week, so I just waited. It shows Ivory getting out of the car and bantering with a couple of girls in the parking lot. He seems to walk with a swagger as he puffs on his cigarette. I shed the beard and went inside for a beer at the bar and waited for him to hit the dance floor. It didn't take long for him to catch up with one of the parking lot girls and shake a leg."

"I see," the judge mused.

"And lastly, I followed him to the park on every Wednesday evening, where he played basketball with no apparent infirmities. His mother would drop him off and pick him up about three hours later. He spent a good deal of time off court and inside his friend's car. I wasn't getting paid to see what he was doing, but I do have time-lapsed footage of him being there in the car."

The judge looked at Jay and asked, "Do you think what they were doing was illegal?"

Jay nodded and said, "I suspect that it was."

The judge stood up and walked to the door. He opened it and said to the group, "I have seen enough. I'll let you know when we reconvene."

Jack Edwards was the last to leave, and as he passed the judge, he heard him mutter, "Sneaky bastard." Jack looked up and acknowledged the remark by locking his bright blue eyes with those of the judge. Then, Jack took on a serious look and followed behind his peers.

At exactly one o'clock, the judge addressed the court by saying, "During the lunch break, I have had the opportunity to view and evaluate the video that the defense has produced. Suffice it to say that it is factual that Ivory Franklin has been able to walk unaided and he has had no apparent need for the wheelchair or the urine bag. However, I have not seen any material, other than the video, to state otherwise, such as doctor and hospital reports. Therefore, I am not prepared to say if his recovery is one hundred percent, or if his use of the wheelchair was necessarily misleading. I believe the video would be prejudicial if seen by the jury. Therefore, I am suggesting to the jury that they decide the gravity of his actions on their own. I therefore deny the viewing of this video by the jury."

Frances James laid her notes down on her table and solemnly stood and walked to the jury box. The room was silent as she began her closing statement. Looking directly at the jury, she began;

"He did it. He killed them with his gun. There is no question about this fact. It was not accidental. The man had prepared for this moment for forty years. He claims that he was unable to stop himself, but he is sure he isn't crazy. He admittedly has had no remorse for an act that he claims to have happened 'sort of' by itself. Ladies and gentlemen, you can't have it both ways. Ray Jordan is a murderer. We can only speculate why he chose this time to actually pull the trigger. Maybe he wouldn't have been so anxious if the men in the car had looked a little more like him. Maybe the stress from being in the big city spiked his paranoia. Who knows his real motivation? We must deal in facts. First, there was no fourth passenger; second, there was no chrome revolver; and third, there were no corroborating witnesses to his story. He did it, ladies and gentlemen. He did it. He did it. He did it."

Surprised at the brevity of her closing, Jack sat quietly reading some notes that had gathered in front of his hands. His chair made a scraping sound as he slowly stood up in the silent court room. He gently laid the papers down, raised his head, walked to the jury box and said:

"I am about to do something that I have never done in my long and sometimes notorious career. I am going to subordinate my closing statement to someone else. I know that it is a risk to hand over the reins of this trial to another, but I am confident that this man will do a better job than I could ever do. Never before have I represented a more innocent man. I give you Ray Jordan."

Ray rose and moved to the center of the courtroom, looked at the jury, and in a clear, unwavering voice he said, "Thank you. I have been in your chair twice in my life and I know that it is not easy for you to put your life on hold to do your duty for the people of Florida."

"There *was* a fourth man inside of the Hummer. I don't know who he was, but Ivory Franklin does. Ivory says that there were only three people inside that truck, but I stand before you right now and swear there were four. Ivory Franklin says there was no chrome revolver either, but Ivory Franklin fired it at me three times over the roof of the Hummer. That is why he was sitting there in that wheelchair throughout most of this trial. He was there to deceive you, to gain your sympathy and confidence. Ivory Franklin would have been unharmed if he had not fired at me first.

"Throughout this trial, my defense team has tried repeatedly to bring up the history of these three men and we have been blocked each and every time we touch on the subject."

Judge May cleared his throat and Ray resumed speaking. "Today, before my summation, Judge May took me aside to make sure that I would not bring up any history of these three men, reminding me again that they were not the ones who were on trial here, and he also reminded me that I was. And so be it. Judge May said that I could not tell you if any or all of these men had been arrested in the past, or how many times they may have been arrested in the past, and for what crimes they may have been arrested in the past, or if they had jobs, or how they could afford all of that high-dollar dental work and that metallic green H2 with the $10,000 stereo and the $7,000 wheels. I am a man of my word. I won't divulge what I know."

Ray paused to collect his thoughts.

"Here I am speaking the most important words that I have ever spoken in my life and I can't talk about them, so I am left no alternative except to talk about me.

"I grew up in a working-class southern California neighborhood. I went to a public high school. I did the regular stuff: weight training, wrestling, auto shop, and of course a few academic classes as well. My grades were better than average but not spectacular. There was one thing that always brightened my day and that was seeing this cute little girl in my 4th period English class. When I got old enough to drive, we dated pretty steady and when I got out of high school, we got engaged. I knew the draft was nipping at my heels, so we decided I would do a two-year stint in the Marines. Before I left for Viet Nam, we got married. So in 1966, I went to boot camp and then I got sent to Viet Nam. I had expected to be a truck driver, but when I got there I was assigned to a forward base camp. Apparently the fact that I had shot expert on the firing range at Camp Pendleton made me more valuable than an average truck driver. I served with the 3rd Recon and after 9 months and 21 days of frontline duty, I was shot with an AK-47. It was not serious. It didn't hit any vital organs and the bullet passed clean through, but it was enough to get me sent to The Mercy, the hospital ship anchored offshore. After seeing that I had already done almost 10 months of my 12-month tour, a sympathetic Navy doctor gave me a purple heart and orders to go back home. When I returned, Caroline and I rented an apartment and soon thereafter started our family.

"I was a welder. I did little subcontracting jobs here and there, after a while I started to make parts for bigger companies. Little by little, my business got bigger as well. All the time, Caroline, my wife, took care of the business side of our little company. So this little girl I met in high school, well, she juggled kids in each arm and did the books and paid the taxes, and filed the forms, and ordered the materials, and called the late payers, and made bank deposits, and balanced the checkbook and on and on. See, we were partners.

"I had been doing small jobs for Atlantic Richfield and one day the materials manager gave me a shot at a big contract. And I did it. For the first time, we were able to start making real money. I bought five acres on San Fernando Road that nobody wanted because it was located next to a chicken rendering plant and built a shop. It didn't take long and we had over 100 full-time employees. Ours was one of the first companies to offer stock in the company to its employees. We even subsidized the stock purchase plan through profit sharing, up to 5% of their entire paycheck. We had people lined up around the block to work at Oilfield Services. Oh yes, and over half of our employees were minorities. We had a broken-down mobile home that we used as an office and Caroline, my wife, was there every single day. Now she had a couple of helpers, but she did payroll for 100 employees, paid taxes to the federal government and the state, and did every other job that needed her. We ran that business just like that for more than 30 years, and then we sold our part and we moved to Wyoming.

"We built a small ranch. It was 640 acres, but that is considered small up there. We raise horses and cattle and alfalfa and we work hard. We have great neighbors. My children threw a 40th wedding anniversary party for us and we had all of our neighbors there. We even had a visit by the county sheriff and a U.S. senator. Like I said, we have good neighbors.

"Our children decided that we needed to go on a cruise, so we flew here to Miami, and we did the cruise, we had one more day to go before we would be heading for home. We had some time on our hands so we decided to go to the movies. All we wanted to do was go to the movies. THE MOVIES! And that is when this whole thing started." Ray paused again.

"I know that this incident has been portrayed in the media as a joke of some sort done by innocent teen pranksters. Ask Ivory how old he is. Does he look like a teen? If Ivory got out of that wheelchair, you could easily see that he is over six feet tall and he easily weighs 200 pounds. And speaking of that wheelchair, you all saw the wheelchair. The one he has been sitting in for most of this trial, the one with the urine bag hanging there in plain view in all its disgust. We know now that it was just a prop, a con, a scam. A lie, a lie of commission by Ivory and by the state. Now, we all know that Ivory, at any time, could have walked into this courtroom and sat in a seat like everyone else. That mess was not his. Please remember the testimony of Jay Elliano, the private investigator we hired to follow Ivory outside this courtroom. Ivory played basketball down at the public park almost every Wednesday night."

Ivory looked down at the floor in front of him.

"The average age of the three people that were found at the scene was 22 years of age. All of them were older than 18. That is another lie by commission. The state knew their ages, yet they let this fabrication of them being innocent young boys get repeated every day by the news media. They used photos of these men that were more than 5 years old in some cases."

"These men took something from me that was vital to my life. They killed my wife as sure as if they stabbed her with a knife. There was nothing funny about what they did. It was hateful and I believe that it was directed at us because we were white. There were six other people walking across that road with us, good people, people who tried to help my wife as she was dying. Did Rondell prank them? No, no, he didn't. He didn't because they were all black. Ladies and gentlemen, they were laughing and celebrating in that Hummer as my wife took her last breath on earth, a woman I loved and respected. They called her a bitch. That is when I shot him. There is no question about that. It made me sick to look at his vile-looking smile. The bastards were celebrating killing my wife, my partner, my best friend, like her life meant nothing to them. People say that this case is special. They say that this case is a hate crime. You know they just might be right. There was plenty of hate on that street corner that day, and it wasn't coming from us. All we wanted to do was go to the movies."

Ray stopped talking and looked down to the floor. He paused in the quiet courtroom and took a drink of water.

Judge May asked from the bench, "Are you finished?" This time it was Ray's turn to ignore the judge as he continued to look down.

Ray sighed and smiled. "We must have been a sight. How much more touristy could we have been? We had on shorts and casual footwear and I was wearing a Hawaiian shirt. Outwardly, we were the stereotypical Northern visitors. They figured this would be some easy meat, someone to intimidate and harass just for fun, but one thing they didn't figure on was the heart of a man beating under the Hawaiian shirt. Where I come from, a man protects his family from bullies, a man has a duty to help the weak and helpless, and if it requires the use of a gun, then so be it."

He quietly walked to the jury box and said, "So let us put away the emotions for a while and look at what putting me behind bars will do for you. I will probably live another ten or fifteen years, and the price of keeping me in prison for that length of time will cost the taxpayers of Florida a couple of million dollars. Since I left Viet Nam, I have always carried a gun. When I am at home in Wyoming, I carry a much bigger and more powerful gun than the little Colt you have seen. I have had ready access to a gun for more than 40 years. How many times have I used it on a man? Once, one time, this time. And it WAS justified!

"Put yourself in my position. Consider someone taking the life of the single person you most care about and then celebrating the death right in your face. Think about it! If you had the means to stop the pain, would you not? If Ivory had not shot at me, then there would have been only one death inside the green Hummer. He chose to fire three rounds from that chrome revolver. That is why he was shot and sat there faking the seriousness of his injuries in his wheelchair. I was under assault when I fired back. Think for a moment. How was it that he was shot in the abdomen if he wasn't standing up on the running board on the other side of the truck like I have always said? It would have been impossible to hit him in the stomach if he had been seated.

"So after hearing me for the last few minutes, do you think that I am the mad dog killer that shows up on the TV news every night or do you see someone who acted reasonably, righteously, justifiably? Do you think the people of Florida will be better off with me in their penitentiary, or with me long gone to Wyoming? My destiny is in your hands. Please consider what is best for everyone. God bless you."

As Ray returned to the table, low mumbles of discord were heard in the gallery.

CHAPTER 17

THE SHOW-DOWN

The judge gave his instructions to the jury.

"Ladies and gentlemen of the jury, the trial has concluded and we must first declare the guilt or innocence of the defendant. The charges that are available to you are as follows: murder in the first degree, which is punishable by life imprisonment; or, if you find that special circumstances apply, then the death penalty may be pursued. Murder in the second degree, which has a punishment range of from fifteen to twenty-five years. Manslaughter, which has a penalty range of two to five years. And of course, should you find a verdict of not guilty, no penalty will be attached."

When the judge finished his instructions, Jack Edwards asked, "The defense requests a few minutes of the court's time to privately discuss an issue."

The judge responded by saying, "Approach the bench."

"Your Honor, before the jury starts deliberation, may we," he said, indicating the prosecution and defense counsel, "please have a word with you in private?" The judge considered his request for a moment and asked that the jury have a continued recess and return in fifteen minutes to start their process.

Judge May asked, "Ms. James, would you please meet the counselor and me in my office?"

She responded, "Yes, Your Honor."

As they sat before the judge's desk, Jack said, "Judge, you have left the jury no option but to convict my client to hard time."

"That isn't true! The not guilty verdict is always on the table."

"Judge, these are good people on the jury, everybody knows that Ray shot Rondell and Demontre. We established that with the first witness. It is imperative that you give the jury a chance to let this man go free."

"They have it! Not guilty!" the judge insisted.

Jack continued, "I have spoken on two occasions about the doctrine of 'fighting words.' I believe that it applies to this case."

The judge rubbed his forehead and looked down at his desk as if he were trying to compose himself before replying, "Those words are clearly hearsay and uttered by the defendant at that!"

"True enough, judge, but is it your place to be the one who believes or doesn't believe his testimony? Don't you think it is up to the jury to decide the veracity of the sworn statements?"

The judge looked at Jack and replied, "Technically it is."

"Yes, Your Honor, on that we agree."

"The man swore to hearing those words in open court, and the jury should have the ability to act on his exculpatory testimony. I cite R.A.V. vs. City of St. Paul for reference on the issue of 'fighting words' and ask you to study this opinion before allowing the jury to begin deliberating."

The judge stood, walked to the window of his office, and peered down to the parking lot eighty feet below. He observed a few groups of colorfully clad out-of-town agitators at different locations. They were near a couple of white vans that were being used as a mobile headquarters for organizing and distributing placards and signs. Without looking at the attorneys, he opined, "Counselor, you have made a valiant effort throughout this trial. I believe in giving credit where credit is due, but this man, Ray Jordan, must serve some time. Have you seen what is going on outside this courtroom?"

Jack exploded. He stood up and leaned upon the edge of the judge's desk and said with authority, "If he gets time, I'll appeal this verdict until I am dead, and I'll do it free forever. You are at the end of your career, aren't you, judge?"

"Yes, I will wrap it up at the end of the year."

"Do you want your last and maybe your most famous case to be reversed on appeal? That's a hell of a legacy."

The judge turned, looked at Frances James and said, "What do you think of this guy?"

She responded, "No thanks, judge, I'm just here for the entertainment."

With a serious look, Jack said, "Consider it, judge. Please read the case law, take a little time. Think of the man's future and also consider your own. Another option for the jury is self-defense! Imagine yourself being assaulted with that damn train whistle horn coming from a car the size of a locomotive; it was clearly an assault on them."

"All right, all right, get out of here. I'll see you in a few minutes."

At 1:30, the judge entered the courtroom and addressed the jury and the media.

"Before the recess, defense counsel requested a meeting with me and the prosecution. Usually, these last minute meetings are done to negotiate a plea bargain. In this case, it was to ask me to consider another jury option. An option that I personally am uncomfortable with, an option that more or less excuses behavior caused by what the Supreme Court calls 'fighting words.' I am reluctant to offer this option to the jury because the statute is so narrowly defined that it suits almost none of the criminal cases I see. Having said that, I find this case unique, and although the testimony of the specific fighting words uttered in this trial are clearly hearsay, I believe that it is the jury's responsibility to weigh the truthfulness and gravity of those words. So, and with great reluctance, in addition to murder in the first and second degrees, manslaughter, and not guilty, I add not guilty due to an episode of temporary insanity as a result of exposure and reaction to 'fighting words' as defined in R.A.V. vs. St. Paul.

"I have been also asked to consider self-defense as a possible choice. I am well aware that more people are killed with cars than with guns every year in this country, but I fail to see where the car was used as an offensive weapon in this case; at most, the car was used to 'assault' only the senses and therefore it would not justify the use of deadly force in return. Perhaps a civil suit for loss of hearing or some such action might be in order, but this is a trial about deeds far more serious than those found in civil court. It is undeniable that the actions of the victims in this case did result in the death of Caroline Jordan and that is no small matter, but to consider self-defense as an option is not offered by the court. There simply isn't enough evidence to support that claim."

The judge stood up behind the bench and directed the bailiff to escort the jurors to the jury room. He then walked to his office with the din from the courtroom echoing in his ears.

CHAPTER 18

DELIBERATIONS

Chuck Schumann was the first to enter the jury room. He had anticipated this opportunity with the same vigor that a young man has on prom night. He had answered the questions from the attorneys in such an artful way that it was very difficult for Jack Edwards to keep him from being chosen. Like a schoolyard baseball game, those favorable to each side were picked to represent their point of view. The prosecution had seated Chuck Schumann and Richard Sanders, both Northern transplants with obvious liberal biases, and the defense was able to seat Moses Houston, the black restaurateur, and Andrew Miksa, a cattle rancher who lived in the outskirts of the county. The other two jurors were found in the unremarkable stack of profiles.

"We should elect a jury foreman as our first order of business," said Chuck Schumann in his nasal New York accent. "I was an alderman back in New York so I know how these things are supposed to be run." Several heads nodded as he followed up with, "Does anyone have a nomination?"

A woman suggested that it should be one of the men, and that comment drew a strange look from the other woman, a nurse named Nancy Del Toro. She was a second-generation Cuban whose parents had come over to the U.S. when Castro purged all of the educated people from the island. Andrew then nominated Nancy Del Toro.

Schumann seemed surprised and disappointed as he said, "We have a nomination. All in favor please raise your

119

hand." At that point four hands went up, strangely including Chandra, who had originally made the comment about putting a man in charge. "Well, that was quick," grumbled Schumann. "It looks like the jury foreman is the lady."

"Since I am the jury foreman, I think the first order of business should be to fill out these name tags. That way, I won't have to be 'the lady' and I'll know what to call each of you. Please write what you would like to be called on your name tag, and then shortly after we will cast our first ballot, so that we will establish a baseline to work from."

As the name tags were passed out, the names Nancy, Chandra, Mose, Andy, Rick, and Chuck found their way to the front of the jurors' shirts.

Nancy said, "I think we should take a poll at this point to see if this man is guilty of first degree murder. Please raise your hand if you believe that this man is guilty of first degree murder." Two hands shot up at the end of her statement. "We have two people here that believe that he is guilty of first degree murder. Would you please explain why you believe this to be true? Or do you want to move on to murder in the second degree?"

"I think he is guilty," spoke Chuck Schumann. "I believe he was guilty of killing those men. He was obviously wanting to kill someone. Why else would he be walking around with a gun?"

Rick also spoke up. "I believe it was racial and should have the special circumstances added," he said, and he looked directly at Mose and Chandra for their approval.

"First degree murder has to have premeditation," said Nancy. "Does anyone here believe that these people even knew each other before the shooting?"

"I know they were strangers, but I just think this guy should have to pay for what he did. I want justice!" Schumann blurted out.

A grunt was heard from Andy's direction.

Nancy said, "Let us take the guilt off the table. Does anyone here believe that Ray Jordan did not kill Rondell

Macdume and Demontre Powell?" No one raised a hand. "So we all agree that Ray Jordan is guilty of killing these men. The question we need to answer is what crime to assign to these killings. Let's examine our options. We can convict him of murder in the first degree, which we have just eliminated, or murder in the second degree, or manslaughter, or not guilty."

"What about justifiable homicide?" spoke Andy.

"I don't believe the judge gave us that option," she replied.

Andy countered, "Yes he did, he called it the fighting words doctrine. I have weighed the evidence and I don't believe this guy had any evil intent. For crying out loud, he was walking to a movie and he certainly wasn't a racist."

"He had a gun!" shouted Schumann.

"So what!" countered Andy. "If I wasn't in this damn courthouse, I would have one too!"

Schumann eyed him with a disdainful sneer and sat down.

Nancy retook control of the proceedings. She looked at Chandra and asked, "Do you have any feelings on this issue?"

Chandra looked down and shrugged her shoulders as if to say, I'm really uncomfortable here and just want to end this thing. She mumbled, "I have no real concrete feelings one way or the other right now." Nancy looked again at Chandra and asked her to please comment further. She meekly said, "I am only interested in having a fair outcome."

"Mose?" Nancy asked.

"I believe a man has the right to protect himself and his family," Mose replied.

Rick got an awkward look on his face, as though he could not believe that a black man could side with this white guy, but he kept his mouth shut for the moment.

"Let's look at murder two. Please raise your hand if you believe that he is guilty of second degree murder." Again, the same two hands were raised. "Please explain your reasoning," said Nancy.

Schumann stood before she had finished her last word. "The minimum he should get is murder two! The guy killed two black teens! He has to pay!"

"What if there was a fourth man in the Hummer?" spoke Andy. "A guy with a chrome revolver."

"Where is he?" screamed Rick. "There is no evidence."

"True," answered Andy, "but part of our duty here is to find the truth and to interpret what we see. I, for one, believe there was another man there."

"How can you say that?" shouted Rick.

"Well, both doors were open on the Hummer. Ivory obviously opened one. Since the two guys inside were shot dead, and unable to open a door, then who opened the back door? Ivory Franklin was standing outside or on the running board. Why would he do that if he wasn't trying to shoot him? I believe the guy is telling the truth! He has been consistent since he was arrested. He has always said there was another passenger!"

"You are a fool," said Rick.

"Enough name calling here," spoke Nancy. After trying her best to limit the personal attacks being slung across the table, she continued, "I think we should all take a break and try to take the edge off a bit."

"Good idea," was heard from the floor. They disbursed into small groups that orbited around the water cooler, the coffee machine, and the ladies' and men's comfort stations. It was interesting to see how the jury members segregated themselves into ideological groups when given the opportunity. After nearly thirty minutes, tempers had cooled and they returned to their seats.

Andy spoke first, bringing up the concept of 'fighting words' again. He mentioned that the phrase had been used several times throughout the trial and the judge had failed to expound upon it until the addendum at the end of his instructions.

The opposing sides continued the banter until a little after four o'clock. Since the passion had drained from their arguments, they then decide to return in the morning. They all agreed that they would make better judgments after letting the ideas and positions in their minds soak in with a good night's rest.

After court had adjourned, Jack walked into the visiting area of the jail and saw Jan and Ray conversing across the glass barrier.

"Do you mind if I sit in? I have a few things I want to discuss with you today."

"Sure, Jack, please sit down," Jan said.

"I expect a not guilty verdict tomorrow and this is what I want to happen. Jan, tonight when you get back to your room, I want you to say all your goodbyes and pack up all of your things. Get them ready to be picked up by my driver later on this evening. Just keep the clothes that you want to wear tomorrow in court and your handbag, that's all. When the verdict is read, I want you and Jan to exit the courtroom to the secure parking area reserved for judges and other officials. You will be escorted by my driver to the car waiting below. He will then transport you to the small commercial airport located less than 25 minutes away from the courthouse. My personal Gulfstream jet will be warmed up and waiting on the runway. I want you in the air 30 minutes after the verdict has been laid down. Ray, I will deal with the press for roughly 30 minutes just to keep them occupied. Tomorrow, I will begin to get all of your personal effects from the evidence room, including the old Colt. I'll check with the hotel and try to get your effects gathered up, and of course we will get Caroline's body transported back your hometown. I will stay in close touch with you for the details. Try to get some sleep tonight. I have a good feeling about tomorrow."

"I like your optimism, Jack."

"Think positive, Ray, it rubs off on the jury!" spoke Jack as he headed for the door.

The following morning, the jury was escorted by the clerk into their chamber. After drawing their cups of coffee, the members sat down to another day of debate.

Nancy suggested that they begin day two with a prayer for guidance. Rick objected right away but agreed to not make an issue of it if the others wanted to do so.

"Dear Lord, please give us the wisdom to do the right thing here in this jury room. We know that our task is a serious one. Please guide us to a just conclusion. Amen."

Rick eyed Schumann with a wry grin. *These people are a bunch of dumb hayseeds*, he thought.

"I thought about this a lot last night and I believe the guy should do some hard time," said Rick to break the ice.

No one responded to Rick's opening volley; instead, Andy proffered, "Did you notice the defense attorney ask about the toxicology and the gun found in the Hummer?"

"Yes," they responded.

"But that was not admissible as evidence," spoke Chuck.

"True enough," said Andy. "Did you ever ask yourself why?"

"Because the judge said it was not relevant, that's why."

"Again you are right," Andy said, taking on a serious look. He looked at Chuck and asked, "But don't you want to know? Be honest, man. Don't you think it would be helpful to know those things so that we could make a more informed decision?"

Chuck smiled and said, "Actually, I would like to know."

"Me too. They are treating us like mushrooms by keeping us in the dark and feeding us bull crap. I think it is important for us to know these details," spoke Andy. "See, we have found some common ground. We both think that it is relevant. If these guys were high and that gun was stolen, wouldn't that change your point of view? Remember in closing arguments when Ray asked where did these guys get the money for the gold dental work and the Hummer and the stereo and the custom paint and the shoes and all the stuff they had with them. He was trying to tell us, without telling us, what they were all about."

Rick panicked when he saw Schumann agree with Andy; it gave him a bad case of indigestion and his face reflected his gut.

"He's guilty!" spoke Rick. "I'll be damned if I will leave this room without a conviction."

Nancy then asked Rick if he had lost his objectivity and suggested that he may want to ask for an alternate juror to take his place.

"Not a chance!" yelled Rick. "Not a chance! He's going down!"

Mose shook his head from side to side and quietly began to talk to Rick. "You have prejudged this man," Mose said. "You came in with the idea that you were going to hang him no matter what. Those who have not tasted the bitterness of battle will never know the sweetness of life and liberty."

The words spoken seemed to reduce Rick to a yapping Pomeranian, so he was reluctant to argue with Mose. He decided to sit down and take a gulp of water to settle his churning stomach.

Then Mose asked the question, "Why did Ray testify and Ivory just sit there in his fake wheelchair all trial long and not open his mouth?"

"Why?" said Nancy. "Because he didn't want to open up his past to the defense, that's why."

Chuck began to see the light.

It was then that Nancy noticed that Chandra was crying.

"Let's take a break," said Nancy.

Chandra lifted her hand and asked everyone to please wait. As she dabbed the tears in her eyes, she began, "I had a brother, two years younger than me. He was a great kid, and I loved him. He did good in school and he didn't get in any trouble. He didn't get in any trouble until he turned 15 years old. He started using drugs that he bought from men just like the ones in the Hummer. We see those drug pushers, and we know what they are. We have to live with them. My brother came home one night at 2 a.m. and he and my mother started arguing. I woke up and came out to the living room just in time to pull my brother off trying to beat my mother to death. He even hit me in the face for getting between them. Mama sent him away that night and told him not to come back until he was clean. Two weeks later, he was dead.

"Was there a big trial for my brother's killers? No, they hardly looked for them. Just another everyday killing. Nobody gave a damn about him. You know, last night I prayed for guidance and today it has come to me. This man has done justice to those pushers in the Hummer. Chances are good that they wouldn't live another two years anyway with the life they have chosen."

After Chandra finished, the room grew quiet.

Chuck said in a quiet voice, "I grew up with big city politics in my blood. My parents were early progressives and from the time I could understand language, they have told me of the evils of the people that were not ultra-liberal like themselves. I have carried those attitudes with me for my entire life. I have avoided associating with anyone who has believed otherwise and probably would have continued that thought process for the rest of my life had I not been forced into confronting my prejudice inside this jury room. I also struggled with my conscience last night, and I asked myself the question, would it do anyone any good to put this man away? I can't see any benefit for anybody. I know this will probably cause my 87-year-old father to die in shame, but I believe I will also vote not guilty."

Rick stood back with a disgusted look on his face when he realized that he was the lone holdout on the jury. "You people are both blind and stupid!" He pointed at Andy and asked, "Where is your sheet, you racist!"

Andy took the bait. He started to stand up as Nancy shouted, "Stop it. Stop! Rick, I have done my best to keep a lid on these discussions and every time we get to a point where we start to make some progress, you mouth off and throw gas upon the fire. You are the reason that we are still here."

Rick started to speak and Nancy pointed at him and said, "Quiet! It's time you listened for a change. I'm going to say this as nicely as I can. You come down here to live with your snotty, arrogant, and condescending attitudes to flee the corruption, taxes, and crime that are omnipresent up north, and what do you do? You try to make us into what you are fleeing from. You are the prejudiced one in the room, Rick. You think we are stupid? Think again. Are we so stupid that we disarm ourselves? Are we so stupid that we would imprison a good man for protecting his family? Are we so stupid that we don't recognize a lie by the state that allowed Ivory Franklin to wheel his way into the courtroom and fake his injuries? What is it going to take for you to see the obvious path that we are destined to follow? They lied to you right there in the courtroom. Doesn't that bother you? I don't consider this a game. This is serious business and I want you to consider it that way when we resume our discussion. Is that clear?"

Rick nodded his head.

Chuck thought, *She just said arrogant, condescending, omnipresent. Good words. Hmmmm, maybe these people aren't that dumb after all.*

Thinking the timing was right, Nancy asked for a voice vote on the not guilty option.

"Mose?"

"Yes."

"Chuck?"

"Yes."

"Chandra?"

"Yes."

"Andy?"

"Yes."

"Rick?" Rick gave a nervous laugh and said he felt like a piñata. He grudgingly agreed to the not guilty verdict.

Nancy looked seriously at Rick and said, "Rick, the judge will poll us in the courtroom. If there is any equivocation in your voice, we will be sent back in here to hash it out again. So, what is it?"

"I agree. He shouldn't get any jail time. I will vote yes."

"Then it is settled. We will come in with a not guilty verdict. They may attach the fighting words doctrine or a temporary insanity rationale to our reasoning, but for us, we are agreeing to a not guilty verdict without exception. Is that agreed?"

They all agreed. Nancy walked to the door and summoned the bailiff.

In an interesting twist, it seemed that despite the best strategies plied by both the defense and the prosecution teams, all of their guile ended up canceling itself out and the most persuasive and influential jurors were those that were found to be people who were considered average and unremarkable.

The courtroom erupted when the not guilty verdict was read. The judge's demands for order were largely ignored by the families of the killed and injured; and as he polled the jury, cries of revenge and injustice filled the air. The bailiffs had to restrain some of the family members from charging the jury, and the fury of the crowd was visited mostly at Mose and Chandra.

Filthy adjectives and threats filled the room.

"We will burn your restaurant to the ground, you traitor!"

There was a fist fight on the first floor when differing factions received the outcome via the closed-circuit TV, and the discord spilled into the parking area adjacent the courthouse. The smell of tear gas vexed the downtown area, and of course there were the ever-present news cameras that recorded the behavior and viewpoints of rioters and bystanders as well. Jack Edwards gave a news conference on the courthouse steps surrounded by four uniformed patrol deputies and had his suede suit coat covered in Coca-Cola when someone from the crowd hurled a half-full plastic bottle at him.

As planned, Ray and Jan made their way to the secure parking lot and into a four-wheel-drive pickup truck with blacked-out rear windows. The driver and bodyguard sat up front and were dressed as construction workers, with hard hats on the dashboard and a ladder in the cargo box. As they drove by the courthouse, they could see Jack on the steps earning his pay. After a few blocks, their trip turned routine and they could begin to smile and reflect that the traumatic ordeal had finally ended. They reached the Gulfstream 150 in twenty-five minutes and were airborne and headed west in less than one half-hour.

CHAPTER 19

THE AFTERMATH

The liberal viewpoints were broadcast all over the local news reports. The Houston Rib House was especially the target of their threats and outrage. Mose dreaded having to go to work the next day.

Before he awoke, he could hear the news vans setting up outside his home. He lifted the blinds and saw the reporters talking with some unidentified protestors in front of his house. The protestors had arrived in two white vans, the kind that community organizers used to transport vagrants to the polling places. He dreaded the day ahead, but reminded himself that he was a Marine and could handle the pressure.

Just then, his wife awoke and asked what was going on. He filled her in on what he expected to happen when he went outside to go to work. They dressed and, shortly after they turned on the kitchen light, the phone rang. It was his next-door neighbor.

"Mose, I called in sick today. I want you to know I will be with you if things turn ugly."

"Thanks man, I hope it doesn't."

The phone rang again almost immediately after being set in its cradle. It was another neighbor pledging to stand with him when the time came. He also said that he was calling some of the others on the street to help as well. In closing, he said, "Mose, we are all very proud of you."

Once again the phone rang. It was George, the early man at the restaurant.

"There isn't even a place to park in the lot!" George said.

"George, if you are in danger, just lock the place up and go home," Mose told him.

"No sir, these people are friendly. They want barbecue and they want it right now!"

"What?"

"Boss, these people want to support you. I think it will be a really big day."

"George, get the fire going and start cooking the meats as soon as you can. I will be in as soon as I can get there."

"OK."

Mose quickly ate his breakfast and started for the front door, but before he opened it, he reminded his wife how to operate his Mossberg 500 shotgun that he had moved into the living room. As he walked through the yard, he stood tall against the bullhorns and insults coming from a dozen or so protestors. Mose was soon joined by several neighbors carrying shovels and heavy pipe wrenches.

One neighbor had already taken up the challenge laid down by the demonstrators by saying, "Leave, get out of here. This is where decent people live. Take your foul mouths and crude manners back to the trash heap where you fit in."

In an effort to intimidate the speaker, a big man in the crowd moved forward to the edge of the lawn and said that he would personally see Mose in hell and that the only smoke that would come from his restaurant would be from the fire burning it down. No one budged at the bluff from the big man, and his threats were heard loud and clear by the news cameras that were aimed directly at him.

"Are you finished, fat boy?" a neighbor shouted. "Get the hell out of here!"

Another neighbor drove down the street and blew his horn at the protestors in the street, scattering them to the sides of the road. After about fifteen minutes of harassment by the neighborhood residents, the protestors slunk back into their vans and drove off. The local news team stayed long enough to interview a few neighbors, but their supportive comments never made the show.

Mose finally entered his restaurant about 10 a.m. The staff worked as fast as they could to fill the massive amount of takeout orders that had come in. They couldn't keep up with the orders that were arriving by phone and in person. Mose directed one of his men to go to the local market to buy as many chickens, briskets, and ribs as he could get for the dinner menu that evening. Their normal inventory would certainly be expended by the end of lunch. As he worked the cash register, patron after patron thanked him for his bravery.

By the end of the night, Mose had taken in over $20,000, which was more than four times his best day ever. He came home after the cleanup was finished and sat before the TV screen. As he unlaced his shoes, he started to tell his wife about the remarkable day he had enjoyed. Then, the local news personality interrupted the regular programming with a breaking news report.

"Earlier today, there was a fatal police shootout at the downtown mall. A man identified as Oscar Powell pistol-whipped and carjacked an elderly couple in the mall parking lot. The pair have been listed as being in serious condition at Memorial Hospital. The wild chase and shootout ended when four police bullets tore through the man's body. Among items found at the scene was a stolen chrome Smith and Wesson .357 revolver.

Oscar Powell is the younger brother of Demontre Powell, who was killed recently in another high-profile case ...

Mose looked at his wife and said, "I'll be damned. We were right! There was a fourth man in the Hummer." She could see that he was greatly relieved at the revelation. At last the nagging question that his mind would not abandon had been answered. As she laid her hand on his shoulder, a tear of respect and compassion found its way down her cheek.

EPILOGUE

Anne Hill quit working at the consulting firm to care for her aging husband. After his passing, she went to live with her daughter in Lakeland, Florida

Mose and Andy became good friends. Mose and his son would meet with Andy at his ranch and together they would hunt quail, dove, and hog several times each year. Andy always had a special table with his picture above it and a free meal at the Houston Smoke House. Andy was liked very much by the wait staff. He was known for his $25 tips.

Chuck and Rick became golfing buddies and have both somewhat tried to fit in with the local culture. It all seemed to come clear on the 5th tee when Rick asked Chuck about his recently acquired concealed carry permit, and what kind of piece he should look into buying.

Nancy has spoken with the personnel department at the hospital and arranged for Chandra to get a better-paying job while she studies to get her nurse's aide degree.

Jack flies his jet to Wyoming between cases and he has a guest room at the big cabin. When time permits, he helps out with the cattle and fly fishes the creek and river.

Jan and Sondra became fast friends and stayed in touch via e-mail and telephone. When Hill and Dale closed, Sondra flew to Nebraska to visit Jan and Danny. Her visit also coincided with the yearly roundup at the ranch. She rode with the family to Wyoming to photograph the event. When the week ended, Sondra stayed at the ranch soon after becoming Jan's new mother-in-law.